OPERATION JUDGEMENT

by

Duncan Harding

Magna Large Print Books
Long Preston, North Yorkshire,
BD23 4ND, England.

British Library Cataloguing in Publication Data.

Harding, Duncan
    Operation judgement.

    A catalogue record of this book is
    available from the British Library

    ISBN   978-0-7505-2808-5

First published in Great Britain in 1994
by Severn House Publishing

Cover illustration © Keith Page by arrangement with
Temple Rogers

The moral right of the author has been asserted

Published in Large Print 2008 by arrangement with
Eskdale Publishing

Magna Large Print is an imprint of Library Magna Books Ltd.

Printed and bound in Great Britain by
T.J. (International) Ltd., Cornwall, PL28 8RW

Author's Note

The first sailors to fly were officers of the Royal Navy. They took to the air, it might be said, like ducks to water. An early enthusiast, Commodore Oliver Schwann developed a hydroplane by private enterprise. In 1911, the long forgotten Commodore was the first man to ascend into the air from the water. His design inspired fellow officers to create the first seaplane and a little later the first flying boat.

Two years later the Great War broke out and these naval aviators played a significant part in fighting submarines, Zeppelins and surface ships. In 1917 Commander E.H. Dunning of the Royal Naval Air Service became the first man to land an aeroplane on the deck of a ship and this exciting and daring feat led to the development of the aircraft carrier. During that war Flight Commander C. Edmonds of the same service successfully launched an aerial torpedo at an enemy surface ship.

Still, after all these successes, traditionalists in the Royal Navy did not take these aerial pioneers, the 'fanatics' as they were mockingly called, seriously. The traditionalists believed that an enemy fleet could only be destroyed within the range of the guns of another fleet. No navy had ever attempted to destroy a fleet with aircraft and no navy ever would. That was that!

They were going to be surprised. On the night of November 11th, 1940, a handful of obsolete British aeroplanes, known affectionately as 'stringbags' to their crews, flew from an aircraft carrier 170 miles off the enemy coast and did more damage to the Italian battle fleet than the British Grand Fleet had done to the German Navy at the battle of Jutland in 1916 – *and all in a matter of minutes!*

This is their story. How some fifty British naval airmen wrecked the Italian Fleet and helped to start the downfall of Europe's first Fascist dictator Benito Mussolini. Aptly named 'Operation Judgement' may it serve as a warning to those would-be neo-fascist dictators who are beginning to crawl from the woodwork everywhere in Europe in our own time.

Duncan Harding
Scotland, Summer 1994

'Victory is not a name strong enough for such a scene.'

Admiral Horatio Nelson

The escape route of Lt. Clarke and Petty Officer Green, August 1939

PART ONE

Escape From The Fascists

ONE

'Irma's Place sir,' Gino Green said in that heavy cockney accent of his, 'a fourth-class knocking shop.' He wiped the sweat off his forehead for it was hot even for Southern Italy in August. The sun beat down relentlessly from a perfect blue sky and not a breeze stirred, even over the sea.

'But it is a shop, Green,' Lt Clarke declared, staring at the flyblown salamis and the Parma hams, crawling with flies, that hung in the unwashed windows.

'Just a front, sir,' Gino said knowingly, giving the officer a wink. 'Old Musso,' he meant the Italian dictator, 'don't like knocking shops. But he knows his matelots. When they're in port they like to get the dirty water off'n their chests, so old Musso has to tolerate them, as long as they're discreet like. And the local rozzers don't mind, that is if they get their backhanders,' he made the Italian gesture of counting money, for although the little cockney petty officer had been born within the sound of

15

Bow bells, he still retained the gestures and language of his Italian mother.

'I've never been in a – er – knocking shop,' Clarke said, his handsome young face suddenly worried, perhaps even a little apprehensive. 'What's the drill?'

Green laughed. 'Well, sir, there are knocking shops for officers and gents, as well, yer know – in Malta and Alex. But you just follow yours truly, sir. I'll see yer all right.'

Green strode into the dark stale interior of the shop, skirting the big open barrels of white beans and olives and dodging the dried codfish, stiff as board, hanging from the racks overhead. The owner, a fat man with a dirty towel wrapped around his waist as an apron, opened his eyes and looked at the little petty officer suspiciously. *'Dove è Signora Irma?'* Green asked brightly.

'Polizia?' the fat grocer asked.

Green pulled out a hundred lire note and laid it in front of him on the dirty counter. *'No,'* he said firmly, *'Amici.'*

The fat grocer nodded his understanding. He took hold of one of the hooked poles he used for pulling down the dried cod and rapped it against the peeling ceiling three times. Clark told himself this must be the agreed signal, in case the Italian police

16

called at an inopportune moment.

There was the clatter of high heels coming down the stairs to the rear of the dark little store and Green said out of the side of his mouth. 'Wait till yer see, Irma, sir. All that meat and no potatoes. She's a big lass.'

A tall peroxided blonde came into the shop, slightly out of breath with having rushed down the stairs, her great jutting breasts threatening to burst out of the tight red silk of her blouse at any moment. She beamed at Green, came clattering over in her high heels, clasped Green's head to that enormous bosom, while at the same time stretching out a beringed hand to Clarke, 'Glad to be seeing you,' she said in what an overwhelmed Clark took to be a pseudo-American accent. 'How are you going?'

'Well, yes well, thank you,' Clarke stuttered, overpowered by the smell of cheap scent. 'Glad that you can help us.'

Green freed his head from her embrace. 'Come on, Irma, old girl. Let's get up them dancers. We don't want to hang around here too long. These days the Ovra,' he meant the Italian secret police, 'are bleeding everywhere.'

'Ovra,' she said scornfully, pouting her thick blood-red lips. 'I fuck Ovra,' and she made an obscene Italian gesture with her right arm.

Together they climbed up the dingy wooden stairs to Irma's 'establishment', as she called it proudly. She opened the door at the top and led them down a dark corridor which smelled of stale food and ancient lecheries. She opened the other door with a dramatic flourish to reveal a large room, filled with heavy dark-red over-stuffed furniture, the shabby walls covered with pornographic photos, plus a cross hung with several rosaries and a big box of condoms. *'Allora – il salone,'* she announced proudly.

For a moment she studied them gravely to see if the two Englishmen were suitably impressed by her 'establishment', then she clapped her hands. 'My girls you will see now,' she said with that Italian sense of the dramatic. She clapped her hands once again.

A hard-faced blonde, well into her forties, appeared, smothering a yawn. She was wearing high-heeled boots laced to the knees, despite the stifling heat, and a black satin corset. The corset was supposed to hold up her sagging breasts, but failed lamentably. She looked at Irma in a bored fashion and yawned again, holding up her hand to cover her mouth, which was filled with gold teeth.

'Renate,' Irma explained, 'belonged once to an English milord in Rome. A perfect gentleman,' she touched her fingers to her lips and gave them a fleeting kiss, 'but very old.' She winked knowingly. 'Need of special treatment, very special treatment.'

As if to emphasise the point, Renate gave the switch which she was carrying a lazy blow against the side of her left boot. But her raddled face conveyed only boredom and weariness.

'I say,' Clarke breathed, his handsome young face surprised, 'do they go in for that sort of thing in these places?'

Gino Green looked up at him cheekily, 'God luv a duck, sir, that ain't even the half o' it.'

Another door opened. A younger woman, her dark hair hanging down to her shoulders and framing her pretty face, stood there. She was fully dressed save for her shoes, but her black stockings were darned and there was a button missing on her dress. She looked half starved and worn out.

Irma pinched her skinny cheek. 'Rachele,' she announced, 'very young. From the country. Almost a virgin. You like?' She looked directly at Clarke.

He flushed. 'Yes, of course, I like,' he stammered.

The girl didn't understand English, it appeared, but she knew something was expected of her. So she pulled up her dress and revealed she wore no underclothes beneath it. She pointed to her dark mound of pubic hair and smiled in invitation, while Irma looked at her proudly like a fond mother might do with a child who was on her best behaviour.

Clarke looked away hastily and snapped to a grinning Gino Green. 'What's the deal, Chiefie? What arrangements have you made with her?'

'One thousand lire now and another thousand at the end of the afternoon, sir.' He cleared his throat carefully. 'That includes the tarts as well, sir,' he added.

'You mean the women?'

'Yes, sir.' Green looked up at him hopefully and at his side a beaming Irma said, 'I'm giving you an excellent jig-jig, *personally*.' She showed her teeth and rolled her eyes in invitation.

'No, that won't be necessary,' Clarke said hastily, while Green looked disappointed.

'Just let us into the room overlooking the port so that we can get on with it.' Hurriedly he reached for his wallet and brought out two brand new 500 lire notes which he gave to Irma. She took them, tugged at the paper, held them up to the light to check the watermark, then apparently satisfied she pulled up her skirt and tucked them into the top of her stocking.

'*Va bene*,' she said and led them to the third door off the 'salon'. '*Ecco.*'

They saw a bare little room, with a rumpled bed, above which hung a gaudy picture of some saint or other, with a tiny wooden table complete with wash basin and jug on it. The only strange thing about the room was the large mirror which was fixed to the peeling ceiling directly above the bed. 'I say,' Clarke remarked, 'that's a funny place to put a mirror, isn't it?'

Gino Green kept his mouth shut with difficulty and Irma rolled those expressive dark eyes of hers at such naivety.

Through the unwashed window they saw what they had come all the way from London to see this spring: the Italian fleet at anchor in Taranto harbour, all white-painted woodwork, and glistening brass in the bright sunshine, with little bumboats and launches

21

chugging across the bay through brilliant blue sea.

'*Mar Grande* and *Mar Piccolo*,' she began, pointing out the two harbours separated by the mercantile port where they were now, in Green's 'knocking shop', until Green said, 'All right, love, you've got yer money. Off you go and leave us by ourselves. Ta.'

She looked at them suspiciously, as if she suspected that there might be something unnatural soon to take place between them. Then she decided against asking any questions. She had long become used to the sexual quirks of men. The main thing was that they always paid. She went out.

Despite the heat the two men now moved swiftly. Green locked the door and drawing out a small Biretta pistol stood there, guarding it. For his part Clarke pulled the camera from its hiding place and, standing a little back from the window so that no one passing in the crowded street below might see him, he started snapping the great white warships lined up below. As he photographed each in turn he called out the names of the battleships and cruisers, '*Littorio ... Vittorio ... Veneto...*'

Green whistled softly through the front of his teeth. 'Christ, sir,' he said as he heard the names. 'Them battlewagons are only a couple of years old and the stuff we've got in the Med. is mostly from the last war, ripe for the scrapheap.'

'How right you are,' Clarke said grimly, as he continued to snap away. 'And the Eyeties have got twenty-three cruisers, eight of them over 10,000 tons and none of them more than six years old. Old Musso, as you call him, Chiefie, is aiming to have the most powerful fleet in the Med., believe you me.'

Green hawked and spat into the wash-basin contemptuously. 'No match for the old Royal, sir. We'll tackle the Eyeties with one hand tied behind our backs when the time comes. There's no one who can match the old Royal Navy.'

'Well said,' Clarke replied with a grin. Even though he was half Italian himself, Gino Green was more English than the English. For him one Englishman was a match for ten foreigners. 'But let's hope it doesn't come to that. If *il Duce* joins Hitler whenever the latter decides to declare war, it won't be so easy to tackle the both of them.'

'Well, we've got the froggies on our side, sir,' Green said. 'Not that they're much cop, but I suppose they're better than nuthin'.'

Outside there was the muted sound of a

band and out of the waterfront cafés and bars, civilians began to pour onto the street, pushed by sweating Blackshirts and *cari-biniere* in their high plumed hats. 'Some sort of a parade, Green,' Clarke said without taking his eyes off the harbour. Now he was busy photographing the docks and the naval fuelling stations. He knew Naval Intelligence would want that sort of information as well.

A minute later a drum major came into view, his pigeon chest thrust out proudly, as he goose stepped at the head of the military band. Behind him and the band came the ranks of the fascist *balilla* youth movement: rank after rank of bare-legged boys carrying wooden rifles over their skinny young shoulders and taking themselves very seriously as the crowd clapped and whistled.

Suddenly two large open Fiat tourers came racing up the opposite side of the road, horns sounding shrilly. Men hung from the running boards, glaring through big sunglasses at the cheering crowd. The drum major faltered in mid goose step. His baton came down. Next moment the skinny-legged kids were scattering wildly as the cars skidded to a halt and Clarke cried in alarm, 'Secret Police!'

TWO

Two weeks before, Clarke had just landed his Swordfish biplane on the carrier *Glorious* and was struggling out of his overalls when the duty seaman had run across the deck, given a hasty salute and had panted, 'Sir, sir, you're wanted over at the *Warspite* at once, sir. On the double, sir.'

Clarke had flung a glance across Alexandria harbour to where the old battleship lay at anchor, the flag of the Commander-in-Chief of the Mediterranean Fleet, hanging limply from the flagstaff. 'Christ, what have I done?' Clarke had asked the duty seaman. 'Was my landing *that* bad?'

The seaman had shrugged and said, 'Search me, sir. All I know is you've got to get over there right smartish, sir.' Then he had saluted and given a perplexed Clarke a look which said, 'I wouldn't like to be in your shoes, mate' and departed.

Fifteen minutes later a nervous Clarke had been standing outside the Commander-in-Chief's office, while important staff officers came and went and the Marine sentries stamped their feet and saluted. Clarke had been in the Mediterranean Fleet for two years now, ever since he had completed his Fleet Air Arm training and been posted to the *Glorious*, but never once in all that time had he seen the Commander-in-Chief, Admiral Sir Dudley Pound. Acting sub-lieutenants such as he was at present, were not in the habit of being summoned to the C.-in-C., especially in such haste. So what in the devil's name had he done wrong? Was he going to be sacked? But C.-in-C.s didn't sack junior officers. That would be left to the officer's captain. *So what had he done wrong?*

'Clarke,' a full captain was standing at the door of the C.-in-C.'s cabin, 'The Admiral will see you now.'

The young officer had stepped smartly into the big cabin flooded with the after-noon sunlight, and stamped to attention in front of Sir Dudley, a big bluff man with a face that looked as if it had been hewn from granite.

He looked up and barked, 'Stand at ease, Clarke, I've got something to say to you.'

'Sir.'

Sir Dudley looked at the young pilot. He

saw a handsome face, with determined blue eyes and a pugnacious jaw. 'The best sort of young British officer,' the captain of *Glorious* had described Clarke to him that very morning. 'Long family tradition of service with the Royal Navy. One of his ancestors was a captain under Nelson. His grandfather was a rear-admiral and his father went down with his ship at Jutland in '16. Couldn't think of a better man than Clarke for the job you have in mind, sir.'

Sir Dudley cleared his throat, 'Now let me say two things to you first, Clarke before I explain any further. One' he ticked the point off on his broad finger, 'what I am going to tell you is absolutely, totally, secret. Two, if you take the job on, you could be in some danger.' He looked hard at the young officer for any sign of nervousness or fear at his mention of danger. There was none. All that Clarke's face revealed was bewilderment, which was very understandable, he told himself.

'I see, sir,' Clarke heard himself say, 'But what is the job, sir?'

By way of an answer the C.-in-C. said, 'Sit down on that chair, Clarke, I've got quite a bit to tell you.' He shoved a silver cigarette box across the big desk in Clarke's direction, 'You can smoke if you so desire.'

Gingerly Clarke sat down in the leather chair. But he didn't touch the cigarette box. He knew if he did, he'd probably drop the cigarette or make a mess of lighting it with his matches. So he sat there and waited, mind racing electrically, as he wondered what kind of job the Admiral intended for him.

'Now then, Clarke,' Sir Dudley boomed, as if he were back on the quarterdeck in a force ten gale barking out orders, 'I think it's common knowledge in the Service that peace won't last the summer. Hitler is making threatening noises again and this time the government won't back down like they did last year at Munich.' He frowned. 'This year we'll have a war on our hands with the Germans. I am sure of that, Clarke.'

'Yes sir,' Clarke said automatically, wondering why Sir Dudley was lecturing him, one of the most junior officers in the Fleet, on grand strategy.

'Now in London they are also pretty sure that once Germany marches, the *Duce* Mussolini, will join in on Germany's side. He's already said that in the event of war Italy's position is already chosen. That damned dago has been sabre rattling for years now.

He wants to revive the old Roman Empire and the only way he can do that is to knock us out of the Med. eh?'

Again Clarke agreed, totally bewildered now about where all this was leading to.

'So,' Sir Dudley leaned back, arms folded over his ample stomach under the white ducks, 'what are we going to do about it, eh?'

Clarke said, 'I don't know, sir.' And naturally he didn't.

'I shall tell you then, Clarke. We're going to knock the Italian fleet out before the dagos can cause any serious problems here in the Med.'

'Knock 'em out, sir?' Clarke gasped.

'Exactly. In the last war we made a bad mistake. We let the Huns concentrate in their Baltic ports, instead of doing what Nelson did at Copenhagen with the Danish fleet – going in after them and burning them out at once. We can't afford to do that sort of thing in this coming war. After all we have to consider that the Japs might get in this new war eventually.' He looked piercingly at Clarke.

'Now then,' Sir Dudley rose to his feet with surprising swiftness for such an old and heavy man, 'just have a look at this chart.' He strode across the office to the large map of Italy hanging on the opposite bulkhead. He tapped the heel of Italy on the map and said, 'Taranto, the Italian fleet's most important harbour in the southern half of that country. But really we know very little about the place except what the map shows. The reference books are pretty bloody useless. And before we can work out an op against the Eyeties there, we need much more detailed inform-ation.'

'You mean, sir,' Clarke gasped, 'we're already working out op plans against the Italian fleet there although the war has not yet started?'

'Exactly. We can't afford to sit on our fingers, Clarke. It's going to be very nip-and-tuck when war comes. No timing for planning there and then. We've got to be like that Yankee general whose name I forget – the fustest with the mostest!' He laughed drily, but his eyes did not light up.

Clarke could see the C.-in-C. was worried. He could understand why. In the event of war, the Med. Fleet could expect no reinforcements. They would have to face up to the whole of the Italian fleet and the vast air armada that Mussolini had built up over the last decade with only one carrier, his own *Glorious,* with its handful of antiquated biplanes that their pilots called affectionately, 'the old stringbags'.

'Now then,' Sir Dudley continued, looking down at the papers before him on the big desk, 'I see you spent some time in Italy as a youth.'

'Yes, sir, when I was four my mother sent me to stay with my uncle who was His Majesty's consul at Taranto. I stayed there until I was eight. Then my mother managed to raise enough funds to send me to boarding school before I entered Dartmouth.'

'Excellent, excellent! Do you speak the language?'

'I did, but I've forgotten it all, save a few words.'

'No matter. That can be taken care of, in fact it already has been,' Sir Dudley continued. He looked up at Clarke's face, as if seeing it for the first time. 'Now then, Clarke. What I shall say to you now is not an order, but in the form of a request. And I shall not hold it against you, if you refuse that same request.'

'Sir?'

'Well, it's this. As I have already said we have little up-to-date information on Taranto, although it's the Portsmouth of the

Italian Navy. I want you as a trained pilot with all the knowledge a pilot must have when attacking from the air – about ack-ack, barrage balloons and all that sort of thing – to plot accurately the Eyeties' set-up at Taranto.' Sir Dudley stopped short as if he half-expected some sort of reaction, even protest from the young officer.

There was none.

'You realise your position if you accept this job, don't you, Clarke?'

'Yes, sir,' he answered a little hesitantly as he grasped the full implications of the job that the Admiral was offering him. 'I would be regarded as a spy if I were caught.'

'Exactly.'

'And I've had our legal expert look into it. The penalty for spying in Italy is death, though,' he added hurriedly, 'I doubt if the Eyeties would inflict that penalty on a British officer. But they would send you to jail.'

'Then, sir,' Clarke said, 'I shall have to ensure that I don't get caught.' He grinned.

Sir Dudley did the same. 'So you'll accept?'

'Yes, sir, of course, sir. I regard it as an honour to have been selected.'

'We had thought of other chaps, but most of your fellow pilots are married, and we didn't think it fair to send a married chap on a job like this.'

Somewhat ponderously Sir Dudley rose from his chair and stretched out his big paw. 'Good luck to you, my boy,' he boomed. 'I know you'll come through. You're from good stock. If anyone can do it, you can. And remember this, my boy, if you are caught, you were working on your own initiative. We can't afford to have any trouble with Mussolini at the moment – the political situation is delicate enough as it is.'

'I understand, sir.' Clarke clicked to attention and then did a smart about-turn.

Fifteen minutes later he had been closeted with a cool-eyed intelligence officer who had briefed him on the mission. 'You'll fly from Cairo to Nice in France,' he had said. 'There you'll hire a car and drive into Italy. You'll take your time, doing the tourist sights on your way south – Florence, Rome, that sort of thing. Take plenty of photographs and have them developed in Italian shops because the Ovra will be watching you all the time, and we want them to think you are just harmless tourists...'

'Ovra?' he had interjected puzzled.

'*Organizzione Vigilanza Repressione Antifascismo,*' the Intelligence officer had reeled off the long Italian words and then said, 'the

Eyetie secret police – and by all accounts a pretty bad bunch. Apparently they try to sweat out information from their prisoners with castor oil at first. Makes them vomit and be sick at both ends. After that they threaten branding.' He shrugged expressively. 'Then comes the ultimate threat, especially for Italians with all their pride in their sexual powers – castration!'

It was just then that a sharp knock on the bulkhead broke the sudden heavy silence. 'Come,' the intelligence officer commanded. Next moment the door had been opened by a smart petty officer with dark flashing eyes and the insignia of a torpedo mate on his sleeve. 'Petty Officer Green, sir,' the newcomer had snapped briskly, white cap clasped beneath his right arm as regulations prescribed.

'Ah good, Green. Glad to see you again. This officer is Sub-Lieutenant Clarke. You will work with him on this job.' He had turned to Clarke and said, 'PO Green is a fluent Italian speaker. I've used him personally on more than one occasion when we've had visiting Italian officers aboard. He has volunteered to go with you as your assistant and general dogsbody.'

'Glad to be of use, sir,' Green had

snapped, as Clarke looked at him and liked what he saw. The little petty officer radiated intelligence and quick wittedness. He knew that he would be able to rely on Green through thick and thin. Instinctively he reached out his hand, though it was not common in the Royal Navy for officers to shake hands with other ranks, 'Glad to meet you, PO. I'm sure we'll get on well together.'

Green had smiled up at him and said in that thick cockney accent of his, 'Gonna be just like a paid holiday, sir, funded by the Royal. Can't beat that, sir, can you now?'

'No, I don't suppose you can,' Clarke had agreed.

At their side, however, the intelligence officer's face remained solemn. He did not share the other two men's smiles. Slowly, as if deliberating with himself whether he should do so, he reached a hand into the left pocket of his immaculate white tunic, and pulled out a small tin. He opened it. On a bed of lint there were two brown pills.

'Let me say this,' he said, pronouncing each word carefully like a patient schoolmaster addressing two rather backward boys, 'the C.-in-C. does not share my opinion.'

'What's that, sir?' Green asked smartly.

35

'That the Italian secret police, the Ovra, would harm you if you were captured. I think they would probably torture you to find out what they wanted to know. Thereafter they'd dispose of you nice and quietly.'

Green looked scornful. 'Them Ovra blokes would have to get up a bit smartish, sir, to catch me and Mr Clarke, sir.'

The intelligence officer's face still remained solemn. 'But if they did, these pills would give you a chance to get out before the torture started,' he said.

'What are they, sir?' Clarke asked puzzled.

'L-pills.'

'L-pills?' They asked as one.

'Yes, lethal pills.'

'You mean, sir…' Clarke began to stutter.

'Yes, I do. Lethal to you. Take that little brown pill there and you'll be dead within sixty seconds – and there is no known antidote.'

Green's mouth fell open as he croaked, 'Cor ferk a duck! What next?'

THREE

'Porco Madonna!' Irma cursed, as down below the whistles shrilled, and the fat grocer yelped with pain. Obviously one of the secret police had hit him. In a moment, Clarke knew they'd be pounding up the stairs to Irma's 'establishment'.

'Ferk this for a lark!' Green cried. 'I'm not having any Eyetie sod dose me with cod liver oil.' He snapped something off to Irma in rapid Italian.

'Si, si,' she cried, as Renate appeared from her room, still clad in her black corset and high boots, brandishing her switch threateningly, as if she were about to drive off the intruders single-handed, 'this way.'

Irma grabbed hold of Clarke's hand as Renate stood at the head of the stairs slashing the air with her little whip waiting for the first of the Ovra to appear. 'Come on,' she yelled urgently. 'I take.'

A shot rang out. Renate screamed shrilly. A dark stain appeared on the front of her corset. Slowly, a look of utter disbelief on her raddled face, she began to sink to her fat knees.

'Bastards – Eyetie bastards!' Green yelled and then he, too, was hurrying after the big peroxided blonde. She stopped at the opposite door. 'A way out for gentlemens not wanting to be seen,' she declared, her Italian sense of drama reasserting itself. 'We use now. We fool shitty Ovra.' She opened the door swiftly, her breasts quivering under the tight material of her blouse like puddings.

'Where does it lead to?' Clarke asked urgently.

'You will see – soon.' She wagged her forefinger at him, as if he were a naughty child.

She opened the door wider and beyond in the semi-darkness, the two Englishmen could see a flight of rickety stairs. *'Quick!'* she said and they went inside and followed her down the dark stairs. Once Green slipped and bumped into her massive flanks. 'Sorry, miss,' he said and she chuckled. 'You like bite arse, sailor?' she asked in high good-humour. Perhaps she was pleased to be outwitting the law.

Moments later they emerged into a kind of loft, smelling of decay and pigeon droppings. 'Watch the wood,' she urged, indicating the low beams. With the woman in the lead they hurried, bent double, across the loft. Behind them the sound of shouting grew fainter. They were getting away, but Clarke told himself that the Italian secret police would soon tumble to the fact that they had found a means of escape and come looking for them. There was no time to lose.

Irma stopped suddenly so that again Green bumped into her massive flanks. They seemed to have come up against a blank wall without exit. 'What's this for a frigging lark?' Green demanded angrily. She smiled in the half-darkness. 'No problem,' she announced. 'That cupboard,' she indicated a large old-fashioned cupboard reaching from floor to ceiling, 'open please.'

Puzzled, Green did as she commanded. The cupboard had no back to it. Through it he could see another loft like the one they were in. He grinned. 'Bloody smart. Right old getaway for tea-leaves!'

'Irma is no fool,' she said, 'now come.'

Again they followed her with Clarke bringing up the rear and closing the cupboard door behind him. As he did so he heard the sound of hurried footsteps. Obviously the Ovra men had tumbled to their escape route. It was going to be touch-and-go.

Irma halted suddenly. *'Silenzio'*, she hissed

and held her finger to her bright red lips. 'We are coming down the backstairs. Now making no noise. We go to the street.' She fumbled inside her pocket for a key. It was rusty and obviously hadn't been used recently. Carefully she fitted it in the lock. It turned surprisingly easily and Clarke guessed it was oiled regularly, perhaps to let out Renate's gentlemen with special tastes in a discreet manner.

Hastily Green pushed a big, red, one thousand lire note into her hand. 'Thanks, Irma,' he whispered. 'Ta for everything. Save a little bit of how's yer father for me the next time I come this way. 'Bye luv.'

Clarke brushed by the big brothel-owner, and reddened as he felt those big breasts of hers against his chest. He reddened even more and gasped, 'I say,' as she reached up on her high heels and planted a wet kiss on his cheek. 'Good luck, Signor,' she whispered, and then the door closed behind him; in the same instant a small man with a felt hat pulled well down over his forehead detached himself from the shadows and said in a throaty croak, 'Okay, freeze it!'

The two Englishmen froze in their tracks. The man's pistol was pointing right at their guts...

The Italian police guard had just handed them their supper – a mug of sour red wine, a slice of polenta covered with some thin cheese, obviously squeezed out of a tube – when the beating started. They could hear it quite clearly down the corridor. The swish of rubber clubs, the thwack of the blows landing on a human frame and the piteous cries of the victims. Clarke's fingers whitened on the handle of the tin mug. 'What absolute swine!' he said through gritted teeth, 'beating a chap like that.'

Squatting opposite him on the concrete slab, which obviously was to serve as their bed that night in the tight cell which stank of urine and human misery, Green said, 'Don't let it worry you.' He nodded up at the grill in the corner, indicating what Clarke had already supposed, that there was probably a listening device planted behind it. 'They can't do anything like that to us. Once the British consul gets to know we've been arrested, there'll be all hell to pay. I mean they can't shop a bloke for wanting to have a good time in a knock – er, I mean a house of ill-repute, can they?' He winked at Clarke over the rim of his mug.

Clarke returned the wink automatically,

but he knew Green was putting up an act that would not fool the Italians very long. He had tried to drop the camera when the Ovra agent with the American accent had stopped them at the street exit. To no avail. Now the camera and its incriminating photos were in the possession of the secret police. As soon as they had the prints developed, which they surely would, the Italians would know what their mission in Taranto had been. He took a gloomy sip of the sour red wine. In twenty-four hours at the most the real trouble would start for the two of them.

He crossed the little cell, skirting the 'piss bucket', as Green called it, and sat down on the hard concrete next to the petty officer. 'Listen,' he whispered into the other man's ear, 'we've got to get out of here before tomorrow or we're sunk. By then they will have developed those photos.'

Green nodded his understanding. 'Yer, I know that, sir,' he said, trying not to hear the moans of the unfortunate prisoner being beaten by the Ovra men with their rubber clubs. 'The only way I can see is to bribe one of the screws. Them Eyeties are game for anything as long as you grease their palms.'

'But what with?' Clarke asked a little help-lessly. 'They've taken everything from us.' He held up his right hand. 'Even my father's signet ring.'

Green winked knowingly. 'Not everything, sir,' he corrected the officer in a hushed whisper. 'I've got about fifty quid in lire hidden in the heel of my right boot. Old naval trick, sir. You being an officer and a gent wouldn't know this, but us rough-and-ready matelots do get into all sort of dumps and dives, places where they can put something in yer drink to knock yer out. So what does yer smart sailor do?' he winked again and answered his own question. 'He finds a nice tiddly hiding place for his few bob, where none of yer thieving hoors and pimps can find it. Like in the heel of his boot.'

Clarke's face lit up. 'I say, Green,' he whispered enthusiastically, 'that might just do the trick.'

'It'll have to, sir,' Green said, his wizened little face suddenly very serious. ''Cos if they find those photos I don't think Mrs Green's handsome son's coming out of this nick in one piece.' He shook his head. 'Ner, the sods aren't going to allow us to get in touch with our authorities. We just know too much.'

Clarke said nothing for a moment. It was the same conclusion he had come to himself. They knew too much. Even the British consul wouldn't be allowed to visit them in case they attempted to pass on what they knew about the naval installations to him. Down the corridor the beating had ceased and they could hear the unfortunate prisoner sobbing like a broken-hearted child. 'What's the drill then, Green?' Clarke asked after a while.

'First thing is to get out of this cell. Second is to find one of the sods on his own. I'm sure they'll take the bribe all right, but they won't in the presence of one of their mates. That'd be too dicey.'

'Agreed. But how are we going to get out of the cell?'

By way of an answer, Green pointed to the polenta with the thin smear of cheese on it. 'What d'yer think that'd give you if you ate it, sir?' he asked.

'A nasty case of gutache, I should think.'

'Exactly. And what happens when you get the old trots, sir?'

'You go to the heads,' Clarke answered puzzled as to where this question and answer routine was leading.

'Natch, sir.' Green picked up the piece of bread and swallowed it in one gulp, washing it down with the rest of his wine, pulling a sour face as he did so.

'Now watch this,' Green stood up, clutching his stomach and moaning. He staggered over to the door, still moaning, and gave it a weak kick. 'Help,' he said, 'help. I must go to the latrine *quick!*'

'*Porco Madonna,*' came the curse from outside, followed by, 'Use the goddam piss bucket, can't ya?'

Clarke recognised the voice immediately. It was the same little fellow with the heavy American accent and pistol who had trapped them just as they were about to escape. His heart leapt. He might be just the man to help them.

Green thrust a hundred lire note through the barred grill in the door. 'Here this is for you, if you'll help me to a real latrine.'

The note vanished as if by magic. A second later the door was being opened and the swarthy little man in civilian clothes was standing there, with his pistol, peering into the cell suspiciously, saying, 'And no funny business, remember, or I'll plug you right off.'

Clarke winced. The Italian spoke like one

of those characters in the cheap Hollywood gangster movies he remembered seeing as a boy.

Green tottered out and the door was banged shut again, leaving Clarke waiting anxiously for Green's return. When he did come back, five minutes later, his face revealed all too clearly that he had succeeded. As soon as the door closed behind him he sat down next to Clarke and whispered, 'Carlo, or Chuck as he likes to call himself, the little Eyetie prick, will do it. I had him taped as a Mafiosi as soon as I heard that accent.'

Clarke looked puzzled. 'What's that when it's at home?' he asked.

'A member of the Mafia, you know the Sicilian gangster organisation, sir. Carlo worked for a big Mafia boss in New York, Lucky Luciano. Apparently the US authorities deported him for running teenage American girls over the border to Mexico for Mexican knocking shops.'

'But what's a chap like, a criminal like that, doing in the Eyetie secret police?'

Green laughed hollowly and said, keeping his eye on the grill in the wall, 'Well when Musso tried to break the power of the Mafia back in the twenties he started recruiting

Mafiosi into the secret police. They got good pay and plenty of power. The only thing they were forced to do was to leave their native Sicily. So old Musso clears Sicily of the Mafia and at the same time used the Mafia to wipe out his political enemies in the rest of Italy, you know, sir, communists, socialists, liberals and the like. Pretty nifty, eh sir?'

'Certainly, but why does this Carlo want to risk his job by helping us?'

Green grinned and made the Italian gesture of counting money. 'That for starters and, second, he says there's a war coming and he doesn't want to be here when the shooting starts. He wants to go back to the United States and for that he needs money. We're being asked to make a contribution to pay for the sod's passage.'

Clarke nodded his understanding. 'So what's the drill?'

'This, sir. He's going to come for us to take us to the interrogation room in an hour. He says most of the police will be off duty then. We're supposed to overpower him and force him to take us outside and escape. He says if we can get to Messina in Sicily and have something to bribe his friends with,' Green looked pointedly at

Clarke's gold tooth, 'a fishing boat could be found to take us to North Africa. That's the plan, sir,' Green ended a little lamely.

Clarke pondered Green's words for a few moments. There were plenty of imponderables in the plan, he could see that straightaway. But it was all they had and he knew by the morrow the Italian police would know what they had really been up to in Taranto. 'All right,' he said grimly, 'we'll do it. But let me ask you one thing, Green?'

'Sir?'

'Do you trust this Carlo of yours?'

Green pulled a scornful face. 'Not on yer nelly, sir. Trust him as far as I could throw the Eyetie bugger, and that wouldn't be far.'

Clarke nodded thoughtfully. 'Then I think, Green, we'd better make certain contingency plans for tonight...'

FOUR

'Here comes the little bastard now,' Green whispered as they tensed, listening to the sound of footsteps coming down the cell corridor. All else was silence save for the incoherent words of someone talking in his sleep.

The footsteps stopped outside their door. There was the sound of a key being inserted in the lock. It was opened carefully, as if the other person didn't want to make any noise. Yellow light streamed into the darkness of the cell. It was the Ovra man, dressed as they had first seen him, and again he had an automatic in his hand. 'Come,' he whispered and indicated they should go in front of him.

Clarke did as he was ordered, heart beating frantically. As they filed down the silent corridor, the Ovra man whispered out of the side of his mouth. 'We are going to the interrogation room. All the other dicks have gone home. So we shall be safe till we reach the rear door which leads into the courtyard. It will be guarded by a police-man. That one you will knock over the head. Hit him hard so that he goes to sleep. Get it?'

They nodded, but said nothing. Out of the side of his eye, Clarke could see the look on Green's face. It said, 'and he's not the only one who's gonna go bye-byes, mate.'

They passed the open door of the interro-gation room. The Ovra man had already switched on the desk light and it illuminated the clubs and what looked like thumbscrews on the table. Clarke looked at them with distaste. He told himself that the Italians, at least, their police, were still living in the Middle Ages with their barbaric methods. When it came to clouting the Ovra man, he'd ensure he got a really damn good clout.

They turned a corner. Up ahead a stout door, with a grill at the top of it barred any further progress. The Ovra man held his finger to his lips and mouthed the word 'careful'.

They nodded their understanding. Slowly, very slowly, he began to open the bolt which locked the door. Outside someone coughed. The guard was obviously alert and now Clarke could smell cigarette smoke. The guard was standing just outside and one of his hands at least would be occupied with handling his cigarette. That was to the good.

Green flashed Clarke a look. This was almost it. The Italian's plan was to take the money and then go back to the interrogation room, where, he would say later, they had assaulted him and then overcome the guard on the door. After that they were to go to Taranto's main station and steal a ride on some train going south to Sicily. But a plan of that kind, they had realised immediately, would put them in the Ovra man's hands. For he would know their intentions, and that was something they didn't want him to know.

Outside the guard shuffled his feet. Possibly he had heard the bolt being drawn back. All the same he wouldn't be expecting any trouble. After all, Clarke told himself, he'd know that all the prisoners were locked up for the night.

The Ovra man started to open the door. Intent on his task, he did not see the sudden determined looks which flashed on the faces of the two Englishmen. As one they acted. Green grabbed the Ovra man and choked the cry of alarm which was welling up in his throat. Clarke, for his part, tore open the door. A guard in a long black cloak was standing there, cigarette dangling from his bottom lip.

Clarke hit him in the stomach – hard. He grunted. The cigarette fell from his suddenly gaping mouth. He doubled up gasping and Clarke, clubbing both fists together, slammed them down on the nape of his neck. He went down as if poleaxed.

Green heaved with all his strength. The

Ovra man's eyes bulged from his head like those of a man demented. Little strangled noises were coming from his gaping mouth, as he tried frantically to break that killing hold. Green didn't give him a chance. He heaved once more, panting heavily himself. The Italian went limp suddenly. Gradually, very gradually, Green lowered him to the floor, still not relaxing his hold. Only when he was sure that the Ovra man was out, did he relax his grip and rifle through the unconscious man's pockets, taking his wallet with the money and then, as an afterthought, his pistol, too.

'Look sharpish, sir,' Green gasped. 'Get the other rozzer's pistol and his wallet as well. We'll need all the money we can get.' His dark eyes searched back and forth across the cobbled yard.

'I say,' Clarke said and hesitated. 'Do I have to?' He looked at the unconscious guard. He had never lifted another man's wallet in his life. Frowning he bent and removed the pistol from its holder and then pulled the man's wallet from inside his tunic.

Green waited no longer. 'There's a car over there. We'll nab it, sir,' he said, pointing to a big, black Fiat tourer at the far end of the yard.

Clarke looked at the car, heavy with chrome and with a row of unnecessary headlights adorning its front. 'We can't just steal an official car, Green,' He protested. 'Besides we haven't got the keys to start it.'

Green sighed. 'Sir, with your permission, this ain't all aboard for the Skylark and that sort of stuff. This is dead serious. If the wops catch us now, they'll top us.' He made his meaning quite clear with a mock blow of his hand to his neck. 'Besides the thing'll have a cranking handle. We can start her with that.'

Suddenly Clarke realised just how right the little cockney petty officer was. All his life he had been taught to respect law and order. Now it dawned on him that his life was entering another phase and that if he wished to survive, he had to apply the same kind of street-cunning that his comrade did. 'You're right. Come on,' he urged with new enthusiasm. 'See if we can shove it out of the gate. We don't want to raise the alarm starting it in the yard. There's a slope to the road, as far as I can make out. Perhaps we can free-wheel down it and start her up at the bottom.'

'Attaboy, sir,' Green responded eagerly.

'Let's get to it.'

Ten minutes later they were on their way, rolling through a sleeping Taranto south-wards, driving into the unknown with all its dangers, two young Englishmen singing as if they hadn't a care in the world, *Roll me over in the clover and do it again. This is number two and I've got it up her flue...*

Just after dawn they ran out of petrol. Ahead lay one of those perfectly straight Italian roads of the region, already beginning to glare a dusty white in the blood-red light of the rising sun. To left and right there were field after field of vines and in the far distance they could see a huddle of white-painted cottages with blue smoke already rising from their chimneys. It looked the perfect picture of rural peace, but both of them knew that for them it signified danger, with every man's hand against them.

'All right,' Clarke made his decision. 'We won't try to get more petrol. The hue and cry will have been raised by now. It would be too dangerous. We'll shove the crate into that lane and then hoof it. The last signpost said that Crotone was eight kilometres away. I think we'll see what we can do about getting some sort of wheels there.'

'That sounds right to me, sir,' Green agreed eagerly as the two of them started to push the car into the lane, almost hidden by huge vines. 'But not the railways, they'll be watched.'

'What do you suggest then?'

Green grinned. 'Them donkeys the Eyeties use around here are a bit hard on my arse and too slow. What about bikes?'

Clarke's face lit up. 'Splendid idea, Green! The Eyeties use bikes and we've got enough money to buy a couple, perhaps second-hand.'

'Buy 'em!' Green sneered. 'Not Mrs Green's handsome son. No, sir, we nick 'em!'

For the next hour they plodded through the vines, keeping away from the road which ran parallel to their course. There was little traffic on it. Once or twice they spotted cars, but they weren't official. Otherwise the traffic consisted of carts dragged by slow, ponderous oxen or peasants riding on donkeys with their wives walking barefoot in the dust behind them.

At eight they started to approach Crotone, with the fields beginning to peter out, giving way to one-storey houses painted a brilliant, glaring white. They stopped at a water spigot and quenched their thirst, disturbed in their drinking by the rattle of a tram. For a moment or two they considered boarding it. Then they spotted a policeman among the crowd of workmen, which packed the vehicle.

'Better not risk it, sir. If that rozzer starts to ask for identity cards and all the Eyeties have to carry them by law, we'd be caught with our knickers down about our ankles.'

Clarke laughed a little wearily at Green's words and nodded his agreement. 'Yes, you're right, I suppose. I think the drill should be something like this. We cross the town and stop at some café for a drink...'

'Yer can say that agen, sir,' Green interrupted. 'My mouth tastes like a monkey's armpit.'

'We'll stop at a café and see if we can spot a couple of unattended bicycles. There seem to be a lot of them about,' he indicated the streams of workmen in blue overalls going back and forth, weaving dangerously in and out of the cars, which honked their horns furiously at them. 'And then, to use your phrase, nick 'em and be off.'

'Sounds all right to me, sir,' Green agreed. 'Specially that drink part.'

Half an hour later they were seated outside a dingy working man's café, wolfing down great crusty rolls filled with salty ham and drinking the thin fizzy beer, which Green had bought. Inside working men were leaning at the zinc bar sipping coffee and *grappa* listlessly, speaking little, as if they were already worn-out although the working day had just started. Someone was yelling on the radio, obviously some kind of politician, for his words were interrupted by bursts of cheering and repeated *evivvas*.

But the two Englishmen had no eyes for the working men or ears for the radio. Their gaze was concentrated on a pile of cycles carelessly thrown against the wall of the factory opposite. 'One thing about old Musso,' Green said, his mouth full of bread and ham, 'he's scared the wops into being honest. So them bikes is not locked. I don't think we'll have much trouble half-inching them.' He washed down the ham with another swig of the fizzy beer.

'What about if we pick ones belonging to someone inside the bar?' Clarke whispered cautiously.

Green shrugged. 'Chance we have to take, sir. But once we're on 'em, they'll have to be pretty nippy on their plates o' meat to catch up with us.' He finished the last of his beer.

'I'll just go in and cough up, sir. You can sort of saunter across and pick the best. If anyone tries to kick up a fuss, I'll deal with it.'

Clarke got up. Again he realised that his life was changing. Yesterday he had picked an unconscious man's pocket. Now he was about to steal some poor working man's bicycle. It went against the grain, all that he had been taught at his prep school and then later at Dartmouth to believe in: law and order and decency. But he realised at the same time that their very lives were at stake. The people who were after them wouldn't hesitate to kill.

As casually as he could, he walked over to the cycles propped against the factory wall. He feigned a yawn as if he were tired and it was a nuisance to ride off on his cycle. He saw the one he would take, a flashy silver racing job with low slung handlebars and with a metal grip above the pedals to stop the feet from slipping. He picked it up, waiting for the first cry of surprise or rage. None came. He cocked his leg over the saddle and pushed the bike onto the street. Still nothing happened.

Green sauntered by him. He gave Clarke a wink, a mischievous grin on his narrow little face. 'Nice piece o' work,' he said out of the side of his mouth. Without any apparent hesitation, he walked across and picked up a cycle. He cocked his leg over it and pushed it into the road.

'*Alto!*' an angry voice cried from the bar. '*Ladroni ... alto!*' A bottle came hurtling through the air and shattered on the cobbles near Green.

'Christ, that's torn it!' he yelled. 'Come on, sir, let's do a bunk, *sharpish!*'

Clarke flung a look over his shoulder. Angry men were streaming out of the bar, shaking their fists and shouting. He put his foot down hard and shoved off. Next to him Green did the same, standing on the pedals and going all out, legs moving furiously.

Somewhere a whistle shrilled. A traffic policeman in a white uniform, wearing what looked like a Royal Marine's ceremonial helmet on his head, together with sunglasses, rushed into the centre of the road and tried to stop them, his arms extended.

Green swerved around him crazily. Clarke gave him a kick as he went by. The policeman's glasses fell off. He gave an angry shout. Madly he tugged at his pistol holster. But by the time he had pulled out his weapon and aimed they were gone round the corner, pedalling furiously, faces red and strained, but covered in grins. They had done it. They had their wheels...

FIVE

They lay among the olive trees on the hill-side, gazing down at the lights of Crotone and could just barely make out the street lights sparkling on the still water of the harbour. They had ridden all the previous night and much of the day following. Now they were exhausted, hurting all over from the hard slog through the foothills. All the same they knew they didn't have time to waste. Sooner or later their luck would run out. They had to escape from Italy that night.

Clarke finished the last of the bread which Green had bought earlier on, together with a piece of hard parmesan cheese and a bottle of Chianti, and said, 'Well, under your expert guidance, Green, I'm learning to be a good – 'er "tea-leaf". We've been lucky so far so I suggest we try again to-night.'

Green took a slug out of the bottle and grinned, 'Three times lucky, sir. You mean a boat, sir?'

'Exactly. I've been sailing ever since I went to Dartmouth at thirteen. I think I can handle most craft.'

'Well, there's plenty of 'em down there, sir.' He looked at the little fishing boats already putting out to sea, with large carbide lamps glowing a bright incandescent white at their sterns in order to attract the fish. 'What about one of those fishing boats, sir?'

'Like something a bit bigger and with a sail,' Clarke replied slowly. 'We don't know how much juice those things carry in their tanks. Mind you, on second thoughts, they'd be the best cover. If there are Italian patrols out there, I don't think they'd bother a simple fishing craft.'

Green was silent for a moment. Then he said, 'There's only one way to find out, sir, isn't there?'

'I suppose there is.' Clarke got up stiffly and grabbed the bicycle. Green did the same, saying, 'I'll never ride on a blinking bike again after this. I swear that my arse has tanned like leather.'

Clarke laughed shortly. Then they were both mounted and free-wheeling down the steep hill tracks between the olive trees heading for the fishing town.

Although it was well after dark, Crotone was still busy. Men, arm in arm, were sauntering down one side of the front, talking and gesticulating, while on the other side women, followed by old crones dressed in funereal black acting as chaperones, did the same, occasionally darting covert glances at the men. 'Eyetie courting ritual, sir,' Green commented as they rode slowly along the front. 'The men can be right old buggers with the women, but the one they marry has got to be pure and untouched. On the morning after the wedding they examine the bedsheets just to make sure she was a virgin. Right old carry-on if she wasn't. My mother told me.'

Clarke nodded his understanding, mind on the task ahead of them. So far the front was too well lit for his liking. Not only did it have street lights, but it was also lined with a score or so of cafés, all throwing their lights on to the front as well. 'We've got to find somewhere, where it's not so well lit. It's like Piccadilly Circus just here.'

'Let's have a butcher's at the other end, where those fishing boats we saw start from. I don't suppose the local talent will want to promenade where there's a stink o' fish. Won't do much for their love life, I shouldn't think.'

'Yes, you could be right. Come on then.' Trying to look part of the scene though they knew they looked very suspect in their dirty suits and with their dusty unshaven faces, they pedalled slowly along the front, throwing glances at the girls as if that was the reason they were there. 'We're peasant lads from the hills,' Green suggested out of the side of his mouth, 'down to have a look at the local talent.'

Clarke sniffed. 'You might think you're a peasant, but I definitely don't feel like one.'

They turned a slight bend in the road. To their horror a white-uniformed traffic policeman was standing in the middle, white truncheon in his gloved hands. He spotted them and shouted at the two cyclists angrily, waving his truncheon as he did so.

Clarke's heart missed a beat. 'Now we're for it,' he told himself.

But at his side, Green relaxed visibly. 'It's all right,' he whispered. 'He's telling us to put on the blinking lights.' Hastily he bent and turned the dynamo's switch on. Clarke did the same. As they passed the policeman he wagged his finger at them and Green

63

muttered *'scusa'*.

Clarke breathed out hard. 'Don't want too much of that, Green,' he said.

'Too blinking right, sir. Nearly pissed mesen, if you'll forgive my French?'

'I will.'

Now they could both smell the stench of rotting fish, as they cycled to the far end of the front. Green had been right, too, Clarke told himself, the procession of women and men ogling each other was beginning to peter out. The stench of fish was obviously too much for would-be lovers and their chaperones.

But if there were fewer strollers, there were plenty of fishermen about, bustling about their tasks, packing fish into boxes and shovelling ice over them, shouldering heavy cans of diesel for the boats, lugging hawsers and nets, though none of them spared a glance for the two cyclists. 'Let's get off the bikes,' Clarke said. 'We can take it nice and easy and see what we find.'

'Right, sir,' Green agreed. With a sigh of relief he got down from the saddle and started to push the cycle.

They moved for about five minutes, leaving the busier part of the fishing dock behind them. Now they were in an area of wrecks, beached old craft with staves split and rotting, plus a few older fishing boats, with here and there a craft which was obviously still in use, but for some reason wasn't being used that night. Clarke put his cycle down on the pavement. 'This looks the place. Keep an eye out for me, Green. I'm going to have a look-see at that one,' he pointed to a small craft with the usual great carbide fishing lamp at its stern. 'Just give it the once over. It might do the trick.'

'All right, I'll keep my eyes peeled, sir.'

With apparent casualness, Clarke started to stroll to the boat he had selected, while behind him Green grinned to himself. The young snotty, he told himself, was learning fast. Two days on the run and he had become a real tea-leaf. They don't give 'em the right kind of education in those posh schools of theirs. They learned all kind of things, of course. But they wouldn't last five minutes in the rough-and-tumble of working-class civvy street, where it was dog eat dog. He scratched the back of his cropped head. Still, he wasn't too bad – for an officer and gent.

Lightly, Clarke dropped onto the deck of the little fishing craft. The wood was firm and not spongy. If the rest of the hull was like the deck she'd be seaworthy enough to get them to Tunisia, which was held by the French and was the closest part of North Africa to Italy. He pushed his way into the little cabin and knocked the diesel tank which powered the engine. The response was thick and turgid. That meant the tank was pretty full. Again he nodded his head with approval. Hurriedly he went out on deck again, and had a look at the forrard deck. There was no sail, so they'd have to rely on having enough fuel. Finally he looked around for something sharp. He found it in a large cleaver which was perhaps used for chopping bigger fish such as tuna. It would do.

He wasted no further time. He gave a low whistle. Green responded immediately. He left his bike and doubled over to where Clarke crouched. 'I'm not going to try to start the engine just yet,' the latter whispered urgently. 'See if you can find something – an oar, even a plank – with which we can steer as far as the exit to the marina. Then I'll start the engine. At the double.'

Within minutes, Green was back, holding a long boat hook. 'Best I could find, sir,' he said.

'It'll do. Come on. I'll sever the tow. It's padlocked to the quay, but if I can cut through the rope it should do the trick.' Clarke took a deep breath and slashed at the rope, while Green kept watch, praying that no one would come by and ask why they were cutting the hawser in this fashion.

It was tough going and Clarke worked up a sweat, but in the end the last strand was cut through and the little craft began to float. 'I'll take the tiller,' Clarke commanded. 'You try to keep us from hitting anybody else or drifting too much. As soon as we're near the exit, I'll start up.' He said a silent prayer, even as he spoke, that the fishing boat's engine would fire.

Slowly, drifting on the slack current, they started to leave the marina. Here and there a fishing boat chugged by them, but none of the fishermen took any notice of them. Presumably, Clarke told himself, as he squatted at the stern, they took their craft for just another fishing boat.

The end of the mole came closer and closer. It was in virtual darkness, but Clarke could just make out the squat shape of a tower at its end. He guessed it would be manned by the harbour master's staff during the day. But now it seemed deserted. Now they could hear the lap-lap of the waves on the harbour wall and the grating slither of shingle. They were nearly there.

'All right, Green,' Clarke ordered, 'take over the tiller. Keep her heading for the exit. I'm going to start the engine now.'

'Yes, sir.'

As Green grabbed the tiller, Clarke went into the little cabin and, with the aid of the torch he had found previously, he pressed the starter button. Nothing happened. He cursed under his breath and tried again. There was a faint whirring. He pressed harder. The pitch rose in volume. Something clanked in the engine. 'Come on, you bastard,' he cursed, willing the little motor to start, *come on, will you?*

Behind him Green prayed as he had never prayed since he had left his council school. The motor was making a hell of a racket. Probably they could hear it in frigging Rome, he told himself, sweat standing out in opaque pearls on his forehead, despite the cool breeze now coming in off the sea.

Clarke pressed again.

Up above him on the mole, a voice cried something in Italian. They had been spotted. 'Start, damn you, *start!*' he urged, his nerves tingling electrically. He pressed even harder.

A spotlight flashed on. It started to sweep

the marina. In a minute it would strike the stolen craft. Heavy boots were running down the mole and Clarke didn't need a crystal ball to know they were those of soldiers. Time was running out for them – fast.

At the tiller, Green pulled out the pistol stolen from the Ovra man. He flicked off the safety catch. Balancing himself the best he could, he took aim on the light, cursing the waves which were making the boat rock up and down. He pressed the trigger. The pistol kicked in his fist. There was a splintering of glass and a cry of rage. The light went out. 'Stick that in yer jumper,' he cried as up above him on the mole wild firing broke out. Flames stabbed the darkness as the boat passed through a hail of bullets.

Suddenly the engine burst into life. A defiant steady throb. Clarke gave it full power. Their speed picked up instantly. Now slugs were slicing the water all around them. Clarke ducked instinctively, as one hit the glass panel to his right and showered him with glass.

At the tiller, Green crouched as low as he could as the riflemen on the mole started taking aimed shots at the speeding craft. Bent double, Clarke left the cabin. 'Into the cabin!' he yelled above the steady chug of the motor, 'I'll take over the tiller now.'

Green handed him the tiller gratefully, but he did not go into the cabin. As Clarke started to zig and zag, trying to throw the soldiers on the mole off their mark, he knelt in the middle of the little fishing boat and started returning their fire. He knew he hadn't much chance of hitting one of them, but he felt his fire might rattle them. It did. They dropped and started to fire from the prone position. But already it was too late. The distance between the boat and the mole was increasing by the minute and the Italians' bullets were dropping short.

Green grinned up at Clarke at the tiller, his face a scarlet death's head in the lurid light of the Italian planes, 'We've done it, sir,' he exclaimed triumphantly. 'We've fooled the Eyetie buggers!'

Clarke returned his smile, but his eyes did not light up. Already he could hear the wail of the sirens coming from the port. He knew what that meant. The Italians had tumbled to who had stolen the little fishing boat. The chase was still on!

SIX

They had sailed all night at a steady ten knots, sticking close to the coast, for Clarke had no navigation aids and he needed the dark outline of the coast to guide him southwards. His plan, as he had explained it to Green, was simple. 'Fringe the Italian boot and on to Sicily, going along the eastern coast of the island. From there to Pantelleria. From there to Cape Bon in Tunisia is about thirty miles. If we can clear Pantelleria successfully, then we'll be out of Italian coastal waters and be home and dry.' To which Green had said, crossing himself solemnly 'Amen to that, sir.'

Now it was dawn. But after the heat of the previous day and the cold of the night, a thick fog had developed. So they chugged southwards in a sea where visibility was at best ten or twenty yards. 'I know the fog'll give us cover,' he said to Green, 'but it's a bit of a sod trying to navigate when you can't see anything.'

'You'll do it, sir,' Green encouraged him

and then handed him a broken bit of board. 'Your breakfast, milord,' he said solemnly. 'Found it down below. Bin around a bit but it don't taste bad.' He indicated the two slices of air-dried salami on the board. 'Beverages will follow almost immediately.'

'Beverages?' Clarke queried, chewing appreciatively on the hard sausage.

'Yes, sir. Found a bottle of water in the cabin and some coffee beans.' He laughed briefly.' Well, they're either coffee beans or goat turd. Anyhow I stuck them on top of the engine and I hope that something warm and drinkable will come of it.'

Clarke shook his head in mock wonder, 'Green, you're a card, aren't you. You don't miss a trick.'

'Well, sir, where I was brung up, you couldn't afford to miss a trick. If you did, you didn't eat. The first time in my life when I started eating three squares a day – regular – was in the Royal Navy. Never seen so much luvverly grub in all me born days. Now back to the galley.'

Clarke laughed again and then concentrated on the tiller once more. He had calculated that by now they should be off the Straits of Messina which separated Italy proper from Sicily. He knew that Italian warships patrolled the area and that if the Italians were really looking for them, it would be about now that it could be dangerous for them. All the same he felt the advantage was, to some extent, on their side. They had the cover of the fog and whereas any searcher wouldn't be able to hear the steady chug-chug of their engine, *they* would be able to hear the powerful sound of any naval patrol boat looking for them and react accordingly.

But danger when it came, came from an unexpected quarter. About half an hour after Green served his 'beverage', a mug of pale brown, lukewarm liquid which tasted vaguely of coffee, bitter and unsweetened, there was the drone of aeroplane engines. Clarke, the pilot, knew instinctively the plane was looking for them. It was flying so low and so slowly. In fact, he judged it was flying at just above stalling speed and the manner in which the sound of the plane's engine increased and then decreased told him that the pilot was circling and why should anyone circle in fog unless he was looking for something on the sea below.

Green looked at him sharply.

He nodded, reading the little petty offi-cer's mind. 'Yes, it's them. They're up there looking for us.'

'Shall I switch off the engine, sir?'

'Can't risk doing that. We don't know if we can get the bugger to start again. Besides the pilot can't hear us above the racket his own engine makes. No, we'll just carry on,' he grinned, 'and do some fervent praying to the old chap in the white gown.'

'Again amen to that, sir,' Green replied brightly, grinning too.

For five long minutes the spotter plane circled, while they stared upwards anxiously, waiting in dread for the first glimpse of the Italian plane. Then suddenly, startlingly, there was a change in the noise of the plane's engine. Clarke recognised it immediately. 'He's boosting the throttle,' he told Green. 'Giving it power.'

Green breathed a sigh of relief. 'Thank God, sir, we're getting shot of...'

The words died on his lips. The noise was interrupted by the sound of a great splash and an upsurge of angry white water only yards away.

'Oh my Christ,' Clarke breathed. 'It's a flying boat – he's landed on the sea. Quick, Green. *Cut the engine!*'

Green rushed to carry out the order, while Clarke peered through the fog, pistol in hand now, determined to fight it out if necessary. Now a heavy silence descended upon the area, broken only by the mournful lap of the waves, muted by the damp fog. The pilot of the Italian flying boat had cut his engines, too, and Clarke knew why. He and his crew were listening, trying to catch the sound of another engine, straining their eyes in an attempt to penetrate the grey gloom.

Green came out of the cabin again. 'Anything, sir?' he whispered, voice tense and apprehensive.

'Not a sausage – so far,' Clarke whispered back.

The tension was almost unbearable as they squatted there, heads turned trying to catch the slightest sound which would indicate where the seaplane was. Then in the same instant that the white-painted flying boat with the roundels of the Italian Air Force loomed out of the fog frighteningly, Clarke had his great idea. 'Green' he hissed urgently as the challenge in Italian rang out and the pilot started up his engines to cruise in their direction, 'get on the deck floor and listen to me – *quick!*'

A minute later the seaplane, the gunner poised in his little glass dome at the top of the fuselage just behind the pilot's cockpit, taxied to a stop next to the bobbing little fishing boat. A hatch slid open. An officer in a beautifully tailored white uniform stood there in the hatchway a pistol in his hand. 'Up the hands!' he commanded with a jerk of the pistol. 'Pronto!'

With seeming reluctance, Clarke slowly raised his hands, a look of bitter defeat on his young, handsome face.

The office smiled in triumph. 'You thought you escape, eh, Englishman,' he exclaimed. 'But you thought–', his words ended in a yell of pain, as Green fired from the lying position. At that distance he couldn't miss. The officer's pistol tumbled from suddenly nerveless fingers. He stared down incredulously at the growing red stain on the breast of his immaculate white tunic. Then his knees buckled beneath him like those of a newly born foal and a second later he fell into the water with a splash.

Clarke reacted immediately. He was in dead ground as far as the machine gunner in his dome on top of the aircraft was concerned. He could move with impunity. And he did. With one bound he was inside the craft, pistol at the ready. Two men sat at the controls. The first one turned in alarm.

He yelled something and began to tug at the pistol in his holster. Clarke didn't give him a chance. For the first time in his young life he fired with intention to kill. It was all happening so suddenly, he didn't have time to think about it. He missed. The glass in front of the second pilot shattered into a gleaming spider's web. But his shot had its effect. The second pilot's face turned an ashen white. He quavered 'No shoot ... please ... no shoot *per favore!*'

Clarke waved to the first pilot to put up his hands. Above him he could hear the air gunner trying to turn his turret so that he could drop to the lower deck. 'Get it,' he ordered Green who had joined him inside the flying boat.

'Yessir,' Green answered enthusiastically, as the gunner dropped to the deck, pistol in hand. His right foot lashed out. It caught the surprised gunner between the legs. He went down, cursing and choking, clutching his hurt testicles, as if he thought they might drop off at any moment. 'Right in the goolies, old mate,' Green said cheerfully, keeping a tight grip on his stolen pistol. 'Don't think you'll be sparking the ladies for a few days.' He turned to Clarke, 'What now, sir?'

For a moment Clarke was mute. Suddenly he realised he had created an international incident. He had stolen an Italian Air Force plane and he was a serving officer of His Majesty's forces. God Almighty, he told himself, in the old days they hanged you at the masthead for something like that. What the hell he was going to do now?

The faint drone of aeroplane engines made up his mind for him. There were other planes up there, looking for them. He jerked the pistol in the direction of the first pilot, 'You speak English?' he demanded.

The pilot shrugged in that expressive Italian way, *'Non posso parlare...'*

Clarke didn't wait for him to finish. 'Green,' he ordered, 'tell him to set course for Cape Bon. Nothing will happen to him if he does exactly what I tell him. Once we're off the coast of Tunisia, we'll release the plane back to him. Tell him that, please.'

'Yessir,' Green said with alacrity, telling himself the young snotty was improving by the hour. First the wallet, then the bikes, after that the fishing boat. Now they'd nicked a bleeding seaplane. Things were looking up nicely. He repeated the officer's orders, with much gesticulation with his pistol, and with the first pilot nodding his head wildly all the time, as if he would have flown to hell and back as long as his life was spared.

For a while they looked over the side, trying to discover the officer who had been shot and fallen overboard, but he was nowhere to be seen. In the end, Green told the pilot to start up again, as the other plane had begun to circle the area. Apparently in no way concerned about his dead or missing comrade, the first pilot opened the throttles. The seaplane surged forward. He pulled the stick back. A moment later they were merging from the fog, rising into a brilliant blue morning sky with the sun shining like a great blood-red ball. They were on their way to Tunisia…

Clarke was worried and his face showed it. 'Penny for them, sir?' Green asked, not taking his eyes off the three Italians in the cockpit for one moment.

Clarke tugged the end of his nose a little ruefully. 'Well, I think I've got us into serious trouble, Green, old chap,' he said slowly, almost reluctantly. 'We've stolen an Italian plane. God knows how we're going to talk ourselves out of this one when we get back to Alex. There'll be an official protest from Rome and the C.-in-C. won't be able to ignore that. We'll be court-martialled.'

'Shoot 'em, sir,' Green said bluntly. 'You know what they say in the thrillers – dead men don't tell no tales.'

'Bit melodramatic, Green, don't you think? You're not supposed to go around shooting people.'

Green thought nothing of the officer's attempt at humour. He said dourly, 'Way I see it, sir, we're going to be shooting a lot of people shortly. If there's a war, which there will be, there's gonna be a lot of people who are going to get shot. Mark my words, sir, *a lot,*' and with that he relapsed into gloomy silence.

SEVEN

'*Il Duce!*' As the lackeys flung open the great doors, the general in his immaculate uniform, clicked his highly polished boots together and flung up his arm in the Roman salute.

At the far end of the huge office, the Italian dictator looked up from his enormous desk, heavy jowls set and pugnacious like that of some prize-fighter who had run to seed. He flipped up his right hand in return to the salute and snapped, *'Prego?'*

Cap under his right arm, the general marched the length of the marble-tiled floor, while the dictator watched him as if seeking fault, clicked to attention and barked, as if he were a cadet again back at military training school, 'A report.'

'What kind of report?' Mussolini growled. It was nearly midday and he had not had sexual intercourse since the previous night. He needed sex three times a day at least; otherwise he grew irritable and cross.

'Two Englishmen. Spies. Caught spying in Taranto. Photographed our fleet.' The General reported in stiff staccato phrases. It was Mussolini's belief that the ancient Romans, whom he so admired, had talked that way, with none of the dramatics and long-windedness of the modern Italians. So all the *Duce's* officials and officers talked in this manner when having dealings with the dictator.

'What have you done with them, General?' Mussolini demanded and added. 'It shows, however, that the perfidious English fear us.' He slammed his fist against his uniform and corseted chest. 'The Mediterranean is *mare*

81

nostrum. The English don't realise it yet. They must be shown. One day. Soon.' He waited.

The general hesitated. The *Duce's* rages were feared. More than one official had committed suicide rather than face them. 'They escaped,' he said finally.

'*Escaped!*'

The general seemed to shrink inside the elegant uniform.

The *Duce* struck his shaven skull. 'What a people – the Italians,' he moaned. 'They do not deserve me.' He threw up his hands. 'What has happened to them, these English pigs?'

The general breathed a scarcely concealed sigh of relief. 'We have word of them, *Duce.* They stole a fishing boat – and a flying boat of our Air Force.'

Mussolini's dark eyes almost popped out of his head. 'What did you say, General?'

The unfortunate officer repeated his words while Mussolini stared at him incredulously.

For a moment Mussolini's dark face flushed crimson and again the general feared an outburst. But again he was mistaken, for the *Duce* kept his temper. He rose from the desk supporting himself as he did so with both hands, as if he were bearing an intolerable weight on his shoulders and needed all the support he could get. Slowly, thoughtfully, he strode to the huge window and stared out at Rome, while the general waited, shuffling his feet impatiently.

Suddenly, so that he startled the general, he turned on him, and stretching out a finger in an accusing manner, demanded, 'Where are these English? Now.'

'A patrol boat radioed. They are heading south. To Africa.'

'Ah, ah. Definitely not for Libya, part of our Empire. Where else?' He adopted his favourite pose, one arm tucked under the other, the forefinger of his right hand resting on his temple. It was the posture of the thinker. It told anyone who saw him that he was thinking; didn't want to be disturbed.

Again the general waited. From outside came the muted blare of brass and the thump of the big drums. Yet another military band was passing the *Duce's* residence. These days Rome was full of parades.

Mussolini made up his mind. 'Radio Tripoli in Libya. Order max. effort. Every fighter we have is to be airborne. Do you understand?'

'*Si, claro, Duce,*' the bewildered general

stuttered. 'But to do what, *Duce?*'

'Shoot down the flying boat,' Mussolini snapped, glaring at the general. 'What did you think?'

'Shoot down the flying boat! But the crew … all Italian.'

Il Duce snapped his fingers with annoyance. 'The fools shouldn't have let themselves be captured. They deserve what they get. Besides it solves all problems. The crew dies. The English die.' He shrugged. 'No trace of the incident. No diplomatic jaw-jaw with frock-coated English. That is the way we do things in Italy today. Go!'

The general saluted and went, leaving Mussolini glowering at his huge desk. He had founded fascism, he told himself for the umpteenth time, a decade before Hitler. But he had given the holy creed of fascism to the wrong people. He should have ruled the Germans instead of the Italians. They weren't worthy of him.

He took his pen, then flung it down again in a thoroughly bad mood. He rose to his feet and marched across the enormous study, shoulders squared, big chin jutting out. He went out into his mistress's apartment. She would be preparing for her siesta. He hoped she would be naked. Already he could feel the stirrings in his loins at the thought. She was, indeed, in the bedroom, clad only in frilly lace step-ins.

'*Benito*,' she cried with pleasure. 'Have you come to sleep with me, *caro?*'

'No time,' he barked. 'Pressures of state. The Empire calls.' He ripped open his flies. 'Quick! There is so much to be done.'

She understood. All his mistresses knew he lived only for the new Italian empire. Hurriedly she pulled off her step-ins and lay on the big bed, legs spread.

He looked with pleasure at the fine bush of jet black pubic hair and felt himself stiffen at once. With a grunt and a sigh of pleasure he thrust himself into her...

While the *Duce* took his five minutes of pleasure with his mistress in Rome, all along the Libyan coastline Italian aircraft were taking off to search for the missing seaplane. Frantic squadron commanders urged their pilots to ever greater speed. Maintenance officers threatened and bullied their mechanics into greater efforts. Staff officers sweated and pored over maps. Radiomen crouched over their sets waiting for the first reports. All was haste, urgency – and fear. For everyone knew the order to find the missing plane had come from the *Duce* himself, and he who failed the *Duce* would be punished severely.

But it wasn't only in the Italian colony of Libya that the *Duce's* order caused consternation and a sense of utmost urgency. In Alexandria, the great British naval base in Egypt, too, the *Duce's* message had placed the British Fleet on red alert. As soon as the signal had been decoded, it had been sent to Sir Dudley Pound's cabin in the *Warspite*.

There, surrounded by his white-clad staff officers, the big C.-in-C. had considered the signal. It was brief and couched in the new imperial style the Italians affected: 'Air Force, Libya, will be mobilised. All planes will fly. Search, and destroy Royal Italian Air Force seaplane, Number 55678. *Pariani.*'

Pariani, as Sir Dudley knew, was the general in charge of the Italian Army staff. For him to sign an order like that, it was clear that the original had come from no less a person than the dictator Mussolini himself.

'So why, gentlemen, does Musso order out his whole Africa-based air force to shoot down one of their own planes?'

It was a question that kept the staff officers busy with possible answers for several minutes. Some thought the signal meant

86

that the Libyan Air Force had been mobilised for offensive operations. 'The Eyeties
have been pouring troops into Libya ever
since the beginning of the summer when
Hitler started waving his stick at Poland,'
one officer opined. 'That daft business
about shooting down their own plane is an
operational code name. The Italians intend
to march into Egypt.'

Others weren't so convinced. 'No,' they
objected, 'Musso will wait and see what
Hitler does first before marching. He got a
bloody nose in East Africa four years ago
and recently his troops haven't done too
well in the Spanish civil war.'

In the end it was Sir Dudley who said with
an air of finality, 'I think we must take this
message at its face value. The Italians *have*
been ordered to shoot down one of their
own planes, and if it is important enough for
the *Duce* to give the order, what is on that
plane which makes it so important, eh?' He
stared around at the circle of serious young
faces almost challengingly.

But no one seemed to have an answer for
that overwhelming question. In the end,
therefore, Sir Dudley ordered, 'Signal the
captain of the *Glorious*. He is to use his
discretion – we don't want any trouble with

the Italians – yet.' He grinned and his officers grinned with him, they knew the C.-in-C. was really champing at the bit wanting to tackle the Italians, who these days seemed to think they owned the Med.

'His aircraft are to maintain a watching brief, try to locate this mysterious Italian seaplane and find out what the damnhell is going on.' He looked up at the signals officer who was taking the message. 'Now go and put that into naval language while we, gentlemen, go down to the wardroom and wrap ourselves each round a large pink gin. I think we deserve it. It's been a difficult afternoon.' He sighed and rose from behind his desk.

EIGHT

'*Avioni*', the second pilot whispered to his colleague. The latter flashed a glance through the cockpit window. Two tiny dots were bearing down on the flying boat at great speed. He screwed up his eyes in an attempt to identify them. Then he spotted the planes' radial engines and smiled. 'Fiats,' he whispered to his comrade, his face suddenly relieved and triumphant.

Green behind them awoke with a start. He had dozed off, but somehow his brain had registered the word, 'avioni.' He looked out of the cockpit. Two fighters were hurtling towards the seaplane, splitting off to left and right, as if coming in for an attack.

'Sir,' he yelled urgently above the roar of the plane's twin engines. 'Eyetie fighters!'

Clarke sat up with a start. To their front lay the blue wash of the sun-kissed sea, and beyond that the dark-brown smudge of the land. But it wasn't the land which occupied him now; it was the Fiat fighters. What were they up to? Would they try to force the seaplane down? The next moment he knew that was not going to be the case.

Angry blue flame ran the length of the Fiat's wing, as it bore in on them from the left.

'Christ Almighty!' Green cried, as the burning red tracer shot by the seaplane like a horde of angry hornets. 'They're trying to knock us out of the frigging sky!'

The second pilot hid his face in his hands and started to sob, while the man at the controls continued to maintain his course, apparently unable to react to the threat.

Clarke did some quick thinking as the

89

second Fiat came hurtling in, its machine guns hammering away. He reckoned that land was only a matter of minutes away. If they made it, they might have a chance. But not with the pilot not attempting to take any kind of evasive action. 'Quick, Green,' he yelled, 'cover them! I'm going to take over the controls.'

'Sir.' Green brought up his pistol threateningly, as Clarke sprang forward. With one and the same movement, he jerked the first pilot from behind the controls and sat down, stick in hand. The two Italian fighters were surging upwards into the sun, making a tight turn at the same time. It was obvious what they intended. They'd come in from both flanks again. It was a standard tactic and not a very good one he told himself. He waited tensely. They were about half a mile away now, trailing black smoke behind them, but already round, ready for the new attack. He licked suddenly dry lips and prayed he'd pull the trick off. If he didn't... He daren't think that most unpleasant thought to its overwhelming conclusion.

Now he could see the Fiat to his left flank was coming in faster than his comrade. It would have to be him. '*Now!*' he commanded himself. With all his strength he whipped round the controls to the left. The seaplane shuddered violently. Its twin engines howled in protest. But the plane answered. It broke left, heading straight for the approaching Fiat fighter. The Italian pilot panicked. Instinctively he pressed his firing button and pulled back the stick. A stream of red tracer hissed above the seaplane and slammed right into the other fighter. Lumps of metal flew into the sea like metal leaves. The cockpit perspex shattered. White glycol fumes started to pour from the ruptured engine.

'Cor ferk a duck!' Green yelled joyfully. 'That's a nice one sir. The bugger's scored an own goal.'

He had. The crippled Fiat, trailing fumes behind it, began to stream out of the sky, the pilot desperately trying to keep his plane up. That wasn't to be. Suddenly, startlingly, it dropped like a stone into the sea. It hit the surface in a great spout of angry white boiling water and disappeared.

Clarke breathed a great sigh of relief. He was bathed in sweat. But he knew he wasn't out of trouble yet – not by a long chalk. The other Fiat pilot wouldn't just go away. He'd want his revenge for the loss of his comrade.

Clarke was right. Again the Fiat pilot made a showy, very tight turn, smoke pouring from his exhausts, and then, flipping over on his back to show just how good a pilot he was, he came in again, rolling over and then slip-sliding from side to side as much as twenty feet as if he thought someone might man the turret machine gun. 'Fancy Italian sod,' Green grunted, 'hope he breaks his...' He stopped short. The pilot had begun firing again. Tracer hissed towards them in a frightening lethal morse.

Clarke pushed the stick forward. It was his last chance. Now at top speed, perhaps a hundred miles an hour, he hurtled across the bright shining surface of the water, the land looming up in front of him at ever-increasing speed. 'Get ready to ditch, Green,' he yelled without turning round. 'When we hit the oggin,' he meant the water, 'out and onto that beach!'

'No messing, sir, will do.' Green tensed. In front of him the second pilot started to cry and plead for his mother. Now they were almost there. But the Fiat pilot stuck to them like a terrier with a rat. Bullet holes appeared the length of the fuselage. The interior suddenly stank of burnt cordite. The Italian gunner yelled shrilly. He went down gasping for breath, a line of bloody button holes suddenly stitched the length of his back.

Clarke hit the waves – *hard!* He jerked forward nearly slamming his head against the cockpit. He caught himself in time. Just fifty feet above them the Fiat roared by, its prop lashing the sea into a fury. 'Out, Green,' Clarke yelled, pulling himself out of the pilot's seat, knowing the Fiat would be back.

'Sir!' Green wrenched open the door. The shore seemed about fifty yards away. Above them the Fiat was dragging a tight circle of smoke behind it as it came in for yet another attack. Inside the seaplane, while the gunner writhed and turned in his death agonies, the other two wept and pleaded for mercy. Clarke ignored them. He pushed by the dying gunner and headed for the door. It front of him Green hesitated for only a moment. 'Here we go!' he yelled and jumped.

He struck the water, disappeared and came up spluttering, 'nice and warm, sir. I...' the rest of his words were drowned by the roar of the Fiat's engine as it came in again, machine guns spitting fire.

Clarke made a running dive, hit the water flatly. Then, together with Green, he was swimming all out for the shore, as the Fiat raked the seaplane with machine gun bullets. Abruptly the air was full of the stench of escaping petrol. Even as he swam and without looking back, Clarke realised that the seaplane's petrol tanks had been struck. 'Faster, Green,' he panted, 'faster ... she'll go up in a half a mo!' He redoubled his efforts to get away from the stricken plane. Green did the same, striking out like a swimming champion.

Whoosh! A sudden hush. Then the explosion. In a flash the seaplane was burning furiously; a living torch staggered to the door, dying on his feet as the flames consumed him.

Still the Fiat pilot had not completed his revenge. He had spotted the two men swimming for the beach. He came in again. This time he lowered his undercarriage. This effectively reduced his speed so that he could get in some more accurate shooting. Green flung a glance over his shoulder at the plane almost hovering there, 'Sod!' he panted, sobbing for breath.

'Keep going!' Clarke urged in the same instant that the Fiat's machine guns blazed fire at them. Bullets thrashed the water all around them, lasing the sea into a fury. Time and time again they survived by some miracle or other. Then it was over and the plane was rising once again, undercarriage raised. It had done all it could. Perhaps it had run out of ammunition.

Gratefully Clarke paused in the water, panting for breath, and watched it. Yes, it was definitely going, travelling fast, heading for its home base. Within seconds it had disappeared and a moment later Clarke and Green staggered out of the water and collapsed on the warm sand, where they lay like dead men.

How long they lay there exhausted, Clarke never knew later, but when he felt his skin burning through his shirt in the hot African sun, Clarke stirred and tugged at Green's arm. 'All right?' he croaked, realising now just how thirsty he was.

'Well, I'm alive,' Green said, sitting up and staring at the still blazing wreck of the Italian seaplane, which was slowly sinking, the sea all around it hissing and steaming with the heat. 'Not like those poor sods out there.'

Clarke nodded his agreement grimly and sat up, too. Stiffly he raised himself and, turning, stared about him.

The area was totally bare. No trees, no bushes, just straggling patches of camel thorn. He narrowed his eyes against the glare of the sun. About two hundred yards or so further inland there was a white dusty road, running parallel with the shore. But it, too, was devoid of traffic or human beings, the only indication that it had anything to do with humanity, being the line of telegraph poles than ran its length.

Green followed the direction of his gaze, 'Where do you think we are, sir?' he asked thickly.

'Well, that bloody plane headed off East after the attack. Presumably back to its home base. To the east then is Libya. I'm hoping we're already in Tunisia.'

Green sniffed and said, 'Well, we'll soon be able to find out, sir,' he said.

'How?'

'Yonder, sir. There's a milestone and a signpost above it,' he pointed to the right. 'If it's in frog we're in Tunisia, if it's in Eyetie...' he shrugged and left the rest of his sentence unspoken.

Five minutes later, they knew the worst. On the signpost pointing east, the name of the town was Tripoli and beneath it the figure read twenty kilometres. 'That's torn it,' Green said. 'We'll have to cross the Eyetie frontier with Tunisia.'

Clarke nodded his understanding. 'Yes,

I'm afraid that has well and truly torn it. But we're pretty close. If my recollection of the charts is correct, there are no further settlements between Tripoli and the French Tunisian frontier. Of course there'll be the Arabs.'

Green laughed. 'A couple of towelheads won't worry us. Eat 'em for breakfast,' he boasted.

Clarke laughed too. Green was the typical Royal Navy matelot. That type always believed that one Englishman was better than any ten men from another nation. Still a good man to have at one's side in a scrap, he told himself.

'Remember, however,' Clarke said, 'that there's the little business of crossing that frontier. The Eyeties will surely have it guarded.'

'Same thing as goes for the towelheads,' Green snorted contemptuously. 'Eyeties – I've shat 'em!'

Clarke stuck out his hand. 'Green, you're a card and I suggest now that we call each other by our first names. We've been through so much together. It seems silly to stand on rank at a time like this.'

Green looked at the officer's outstretched hand, face shocked. 'But you're an officer and gent, sir. I once read when Captain

Scott was on his expedition and they were all huddled in a tent, ready to snuff it, he drew a line across the floor to separate the ratings from the officers. Said it was better for morale and all that stuff.'

'Come off it, Gino. Take my hand. My first name is George.'

Reluctantly, very reluctantly, Gino Green took the officer's hand, almost as if it might be red-hot, and pressed it limply. 'All right, – er – George,' he said hesitantly. 'Till we get back to the ship, then.'

If we get back!, a harsh little voice at the back of Clarke's head rasped. But he didn't say that aloud. Instead he said, 'We'll stick to the road. It's better for walking than all this loose sand. It's dead straight and we should be able to see anything approaching us.'

'Yes si – er – George, and they'll be able to spot us too.'

Clarke looked up at the blood-red ball of the sun. It was getting low in the west, the direction they would march. 'The sun'll be beyond the horizon in a couple of hours, Gino,' he said. 'With luck we can reach the French Tunisian frontier before it rises again. All right, let's start hoofing it.'

Gino Green made a sound like a horse

whinnying and then said, 'All right then, gee up!'

Together, two lone figures in that vast empty landscape, they set off, knowing instinctively that this was their last chance...

NINE

Night.

The sky was a dark purple, studded with icy, remote stars. A freezing wind blew over the desert. Millions of sand particles contracted in the sudden cold after the heat of the day and gave off a strange kind of eerie music. Not that they were listening. They were concentrating totally on keeping going.

Twice they had seen vehicles running along the coastal road to Tunisia. But they had seen the vehicles first and had thrown themselves into the drainage ditch at the side of the road. Once they had seen an Arab leading a group of camels and scraggy goats. But he had paid no attention to them and Clarke had said to his companion. 'Probably he's a Senussi. They've been the deadly enemies of the Italians ever since the war the Italian Army fought with them back in the twenties.'

But now nothing stirred. It was as if they were all alone in the world, the last surviving members of the human race. Clarke told himself that couldn't be the case. They were pretty near the frontier now by his calculations and at this time with war in the air between Germany and Italy, on the one side, and the allies, Britain and France, on the other, there was sure to be a lot of Italian troops manning the border between Tunisia and Libya.

'All right, Gino,' he said. 'Let's take a break. It's no use going at it head on. We'll need to be on our toes once we enter the border region.'

'Suits me, George. I'm fair knackered as it is.' He sat down suddenly and Clarke did the same, saying, 'Dig a bit of a hole in the sand. Down below the surface – it'll still be warm from the sun and besides it keeps you out of the wind.'

'Right-o,' Gino said, as Clarke started scraping out the sand with his bare hands shivering as he did so, for the wind was really icy; finding a pebble as he dug, he put it in his mouth to ease his terrible thirst.

Five minutes later they were huddled side

by side in their holes, collars turned up about their ears, teeth chattering still but definitely warmer than they had been ever since the sun had set. 'My guess is,' Clarke said slowly and carefully, as if he was thinking out the words as he spoke, 'that we've got about another three hours till dawn. Now the last signpost we saw stated fifteen kilometres to the frontier.'

'That's right – er – George,' Gino agreed and Clarke noted the other man still hesitated to use his first name.

'So if we can clock up about six to seven kilometres an hour after we've had a bit of a rest,' Clarke went on, 'we should reach the frontier just before dawn. And you know what it's like near the end of a watch on board ship, matelots start to get a bit bog-eyed and not as observant as they should be. I should imagine it's exactly the same with the brown jobs,' he meant the army.

'Yer, they'll be wondering when their relief is going to turn up and whether there'll be any char left in the bucket and that sort of thing. Mind on other things…' He stopped short.

'What is it?' Clarke asked in sudden alarm.

By way of answer, the little cockney petty

officer cocked his head to one side, hand behind his ear so that he could hear better. 'There's something out there,' he whispered tensely.

'A wild animal?'

'Not out here. We know that. There'd be nothing for the poor wild sods to eat – or drink.'

Together, hearts racing like trip hammers, the two fugitives strained to make out what was out there in the desert, knowing without saying that it could only be one of two things: some wandering Arab or the enemy!

Suddenly, startlingly, they saw the camels, a line of a dozen of them outlined in stark black by the ghostly silver light of the stars. Gino Green breathed a sigh of relief, 'Wogs after all,' he said. 'I thought it might be the Eyeties…' he stopped short. 'Christ!' He exclaimed.

Leading the little patrol, torch suddenly flashing on, there was a man in a long white cloak, peaked hat cocked rakishly on the side of his head and the beam of his torch was aimed directly at the two Englishmen crouched in their shallow holes.

'Native levies,' Clarke said in disgust, 'under an Italian officer.'

There was the unmistakeable threatening noise of rifle bolts being drawn back as the officer said in perfect English, 'I think you are the two chaps we've been looking for. Now will you have the goodness to raise your hands. My chaps tend to be a little excitable and trigger-happy...'

Slowly, miserably, the two fugitives got to their feet and with a feeling of absolute despair, raised their hands...

Dawn. They squatted around a fire of camel thorn, as the native soldiers brewed sticky, sugary green tea and the three of them, the two Englishmen and the handsome Italian officer drank strong black coffee, laced with grappa. 'Awfully bad luck for you chaps,' the young officer was saying in the accents of a well-bred, upper class Englishman, for he had, after all, been educated, in part, at Eton. 'So close and then pipped at the post. You're only eight kilometres from French territory, you know. Bad show, what?'

Gino took a swallow of the strong coffee and remained stony-faced, as he watched the native troops throw yet more sugar in the tea which they were boiling for the second time. They might be wogs, he told himself, but they were well armed and looked determined. Besides their own weapons had been confiscated.

Clarke, for his part, said, 'What's the drill?'

'Drill, old boy?' The handsome young officer, with the flashing dark eyes and trim film-star moustache, smiled at him and answered, 'Well, first I hand you to my commandant. He'll hand you over to the secret police. Then I suppose,' he shrugged carelessly, 'they'll shoot you as spies. They usually do, you know. Rotten bad luck.'

'Yes, rotten bad luck,' Clarke agreed, but irony was wasted on the young Italian officer. Besides he was so pleased to have captured the two escapees when they were so close to freedom that he didn't even notice.

'Caused quite a stir, you did, you know. Had the chaps at HQ thoroughly rattled and all that. The senior officers were really wetting their knickers. I say, I am being a bad host. What about another cup of this absolutely terrible coffee?'

Miserably Clarke shook his head, but Gino Green, as always with one eye to the main chance, said, 'What about a bit of grub, sir? I'm famished.'

'See what I can do. I took a liking to saus-ages when I was at Eton. Periodically I have tinned sausages sent to me by *Fortnum and Mason.* I'll ask my man to fish some out–' He stopped and frowned, as he looked up at the sun. It was like a copper coin glimpsed at the bottom of a scummy pool. It was becoming hotter by the minute, too, and not a breeze stirred, although they were only a few miles away from the sea. He shuddered a little. He knew the signs.

'What's up, sir?' Gino asked, tinned sausages forgotten, keen eyes searching the Italian's handsome face.

'Might have a spot of bother, soon.'

'Bother?'

'Yes, the signs all indicate a sandstorm. I think you'll have to do without those splendid sausages.' He turned to the natives, still drinking their sticky green tea, dark faces expressionless. He said something in Arabic. They touched their foreheads in salute, drank their tea, and moved to their camels in that lazy manner of Arabs, who knew nothing in life was worth hurrying for.

'You'll have to tag along on foot,' the officer said. 'We'll go slow – walking pace. I'd like to get you to HQ before the storm hits us. They can be quite beastly, you know.'

Clarke didn't know, but he knew a chance when he saw one. He flashed a look at Gino

Green. The latter winked slightly. He'd got the message as well. The storm might be their last chance.

Now they plodded on behind the camels, their faces lathered in sweat, clothes black with perspiration and clinging to them unpleasantly. The sun had vanished now and the wind had been rising steadily for the last hour. Visibility had been reduced dramatically and Clarke and Green at the end of the column could barely see the young Italian officer who led it.

Despite the overwhelming heat, Clarke prayed fervently for the storm to come. For already they were passing the Italian border positions, sandbagged weapon pits surrounded by rusting barbed wire, or small concrete pillboxes and from the sounds coming from the latter, he knew they were occupied. It wouldn't be long now, he told himself, before they arrived at the Italian headquarters and then there'd be no hope for them. They'd be shot, he knew that well enough. Hadn't the officer said so?

Another quarter of an hour passed. They went by an Italian laager. Soldiers were battling against the wind to throw tarpaulins over their vehicles, staking the ends down with tent pegs and hammers. No one paid the slightest attention to the patrol. All were intent, obviously, in getting ready for the storm to come.

Clarke dug his nails into the palms of his sweating hands. 'Come on,' he willed the storm to come, 'come on, damn you. *Now!*' he hissed to himself. It could only be a matter of minutes before they came to the Italian HQ. All the installations about them indicated that they were approaching the centre of this Italian activity.

The first tremendous gust of wind hit them like a blow from a fist. Just before he disappeared in the streaming rush of sand, the Italian in the lead was stopped dead in his tracks by the impact. Clarke grabbed hold of his companion's hand. 'Hold on, Gino,' he yelled, the words were being torn from his mouth by the wind, 'we mustn't be separated … this is our … chance … OK?'

Already disappearing into the howling yellow cloud, the Arabs were dropping their camels to their forelegs and then wedging themselves in their lee, trying to find some protection from that terrible cutting wind, filled with sand. No one took the slightest notice of the two prisoners and indeed in a flash everyone else had vanished.

Clarke and Green, heads bent, bodies

doubled, blundered a few yards away from the road and then they could go no further, as the wind struck them at one hundred miles an hour. It was like a wall of hot, sharp razor blades, slashing at their faces with lethal ferocity. Sand particles struck through their thin clothing. They opened their mouths to howl with pain, but couldn't. The impact was too tremendous.

Breathing became terribly difficult. The howling, hellish fog of sand snatched the very air from their lungs. They coughed and choked like ancient asthmatics in their death throes. Above their heads the ululating threnody rose to an ever louder pitch. It screamed and shrieked like some terrible banshee. It had crossed a thousand miles of desert to seize them and it was not to be denied its victims...

Time and time again it battered and beat them. Once for a moment, a fleeting moment, when it dropped, Clarke raised his head. The native soldiers had vanished. Or were those sand mounds, looking like new graves, the soldiers and their camels? Next moment the wind came shrieking in once more and he ducked fearfully.

With renewed force the sandstorm came at them. It was a personal thing, as if some god on high had ordained that these puny mortals should be wiped off the face of the earth for their temerity in penetrating his burning kingdom. With all his remaining strength, Clarke clung to Gino Green, as if they were desperate lovers in the throes of one great final passion.

The dread howling seemed to go on for ever. Clarke could feel how they were being buried in sand. Vigorously he fought to rid himself of the weight. Gino did the same. They had to be ready to make a break for it, as soon as the severity of the storm had abated a little. *They had to.*

But gradually Clarke started to detect a change in the shrieking of the wind. It was beginning to be replaced by a kind of softer dirge. He tugged at Gino's hand and raised his head. The sand still flew thickly, but with less speed. He shook his head. The sand dropped from it. He sucked in a breath of air which seemed no longer so burning hot. Visibility was still virtually nil. He had no idea of what direction to go. But go they must, he knew that. 'Gino,' he hissed into the other man's ear. 'This is it... Let's go!'

TEN

Three shots rang out, one after another, deliberate and dogmatic. The two men, slogging their way through the camel thorn scrub, their clothes and bodies ripped and torn by the fierce spikes, knew what that meant. It was a signal. Their disappearance had been discovered. The young Italian officer was alerting the area. Soon the place would be swarming with Italians searching for them. Gasping, bleeding, faces glazed with sweat, eyes bulging from their heads like men demented, they pushed on.

To their front in the far distance, a signal shell exploded in the sky in a glare of green. It was followed by another and another.

'What's that in aid of, George?' Gino gasped from a mouth that was gaping and slack like that of some village idiot.

Despite his exhaustion, Clarke's heart leapt. 'French… French recognition signal… Seen it before … on exercise with the French … means impending attack… Perhaps they think the Italians are going to attack them…

The firing, I mean.'

'D'yer mean, that … the frogs is over there?' There was new hope in the little cockney's voice.

'Yes, I do … come on. Into that wadi… Might give us a little cover.'

Just in time they scrambled into the depression, ringed in on two sides by steep walls, running roughly parallel to what Clarke took to be the French Tunisian frontier. For to the right a biplane was rising into the sky; and they knew why. It was an Italian spotter plane sent to look for them.

Now they pushed on more quickly, un-hampered by the camel thorn. The going was still rough though. The wadi was lit-tered with football-sized rocks and it was a matter of stumbling over or between them. The effort lathered them in sweat, but they persisted, their lungs gasping like pairs of cracked leathern bellows. For they knew now that the frontier could be only a matter of a couple of hundred yards or so away.

The biplane, sounding like an old sewing machine, came in closer. Clarke flung a glance over his shoulder. He caught a quick flash of glass in the sunlight. Someone up there was using binoculars. Yes, they were definitely hunting for them. 'Duck, Gino,'

111

he cried urgently, as the biplane swept over the right wall of the wadi. They fell as one, pressing their faces into the rocky earth.

With maddening slowness the biplane spotter started to cruise the length of the wadi. 'Come on, come on,' Clarke moaned angrily to himself. 'Get the hell out of here.' He knew that time was running out fast. He wanted rid of the spotter. Then it was gone and they were moving once more, panting in their haste, following the curve of the wadi, knowing that soon they would have to leave the cover of its rocky depths for it was curving away from where they guessed the French frontier to be.

The rickety drone of the spotter plane died away and Clarke decided that they had gone as far as they dare in the wadi. 'All right, Gino, we'll have to get up that, I'm afraid.' He stared at the rock wall, which looked pretty sheer closer to the top of the wadi.

'I'm afraid, George. Ain't got much of a head for heights. But still, here goes.' He put his foot on the nearest rock outcrop and reaching up until he found a handhold, he levered himself up with a grunt. Clarke did the same.

It was tough going and slow work. For six

yards they crawled through the sheer hell of clumps of murderous camel thorn which tore and ripped at their flesh. Once Clarke hung on with the tips of his fingers and no foothold, caught by a patch of thorn which had ripped into his shirt. Desperately he twisted and turned, trying to release himself, the sweat pouring down his contorted face. As one barbed thorn gave way, another lashed forward against his face tearing the flesh in a dozen places. He stifled his cry of agony, feeling the hot coppery blood pouring into his mouth. In the end he freed himself and together with Gino started up an almost sheer rock wall, grateful for any handhold and the clumps of coarse desert grass which were strong enough to hold the weight of a man.

Once Gino poked the toe of his shoe in a hole in the rock, panting feverishly as he did so. He reached his hand up gingerly for a fingerhold. Suddenly the foothold gave. His hand slipped. The rock ripped off two fingernails. A wave of an unbearable, electric pain shot through his skinny body. He thrust his face into the rock wall to stifle his cries. Still they went on.

They had almost reached the top when the little spotter plane came back. This time it didn't miss them. They were clearly visible, spreadeagled on the rock face. Clarke craned his neck round. He could see the dark outlines of the pilot and observer quite clearly behind the gleaming perspex of the canopy. Was the plane armed? They'd be sitting ducks on the cliff. It wasn't. Next moment a red signal flare arched into the sky and exploded in a burst of unnatural red light. The plane was signalling to the searchers.

In a frenzy of despair and energy, they scrambled up the remaining few yards of the cliff. For a moment they lay on the lip of the wadi, gasping for breath. But already they could hear the shouts from far off – and the plane was coming back to observe their movements.

Clarke dragged Gino to his feet. The little cockney looked an awful mess. His clothing was ripped and torn and stained with fresh blood. His face was a mess of scratches. But then, Clarke told himself, he probably didn't look much better. With legs that seemed strangely rubbery, Clarke staggered forward, dragging Gino with him.

Up ahead lay a line of barbed wire with what looked like empty food tins attached to the wire. That would be the wire – the cans would be a primitive kind of warning device to detect intruders. It had to be the French frontier. 'Come on, Gino,' he croaked. 'That's it.'

'All right, George... Do my best.' Gino broke into a shambling run. Behind them on the other side of the wadi, the Italians were setting up a light machine gun. It wouldn't be long before they opened fire. Before them a solitary soldier, rifle slung over his shoulder patrolled the Italian side of the wire, unaware of what was happening behind him.

'Nobble him, George,' Gino gasped. 'Only way. Then over the wi–' the words died on his lips. The sentry was turning. His face registered a kind of shocked indignation. He started to fumble with the strap of his rifle. Clarke didn't give him a chance to unsling it. With almost the last of his strength, he slammed his fist into the soldier's face.

The man screamed shrilly. Blood arced from his broken nose in a scarlet stream. He went down, still holding his nose. Gino kicked him as he staggered. The sentry keeled over on one side and moaned piteously.

They ran on. Across on the other side of the wadi, an Italian dropped behind the light machine gun. He jerked up the butt. An officer yelled out the range. Tracer flew from the muzzle. All about the running men, the bullets kicked up the sand. They kept going. There was no alternative. They zig-zagged, slugs missing their flying heels by inches. Panting crazily, faces lathered in sweat, Clarke knew their luck wouldn't hold out much longer.

A kind of half-concealed bunker appeared to their front, with beyond it, the wire only a hundred yards or so away. A bareheaded man appeared. In his hand he held a stick grenade. He shouted something they couldn't understand in Italian. He raised his arm, dark, hairy and muscular. He was going to throw the grenade at them. Behind, the machine gun ceased firing. The gunner obviously didn't want to hit his own comrade. Perhaps he told himself the grenade thrower couldn't miss at that range.

The running men could see the thrower's face quite clearly. His expression was a mixture of anger and animal strength. He knew he couldn't miss; that he was going to blast these two men running towards him out of this world in one moment more.

'*En avant!*' The rallying cry in French took the two fugitives completely by surprise. '*A l'attaque.*' Suddenly there they were, riding over the sand, Spahis in their long woollen cloaks, with at their head an officer with his kepi tilted to one side and a cigar stuck in the corner of his mouth.

The grenade-thrower hesitated. He wondered what he should do. By the time he had come to a decision, if he ever did, it was too late. A rifle cracked. He doubled up, back blasted open. The Italian hung there for a moment, as the stick grenade fell from suddenly nerveless fingers. In a flash of scarlet flame it exploded at his feet. His legs disappeared in a welter of bloody gore. He dropped to the stumps, the bone shining through the scarlet like polished ivory. For a moment he seemed to be attempting to walk on them. Then he gave a little sigh, as if he were suddenly tired and urgently needed to sleep. He fell face forward in the sand and died – quietly.

The Spahis, carried away by the sudden killing, drew their sabres, dark faces glistening with sweat and excitement, charging forward at full gallop, the air full of the harsh breathing of the horses, the clank of stirrups and bits, the throaty cries of the native cavalry.

On the wadi ridge opposite the Italians panicked. The gunner kicked his machine gun into the gully. Suddenly, he, all of them, were running, crying, *'Francesi ... Franc-esi...!'*

Capitaine Le Blanc drew off his kepi and wiped the sweat off his brow. He smiled down at the two fugitives. In heavily accented English, he said, 'The Macaronis run... It is typical for them.' He indicated the fleeing Italians with his whip, while all around him his Spahis looked angrily at the departing Italians beyond the wire, as if they would have given their very lives to have ridden them down.

'Thank you very much,' Clarke said, feeling very weary, as if a tap had been opened and all strength had fled his body.

'Saved our bacon, sir,' Gino Green chimed in.

'Ah the famous English bacon and eggs,' Capitaine Le Blanc said and looked puzzled. 'No, but this night you shall have cous-cous, prepared by my men.' He touched his fingers to his lips. *'Formidable.'* Then his face grew grave. 'You know this day – what day this is?'

Clarke scratched the back of his head. 'I'm afraid I've lost track of time a little, Captain.' He considered for a moment, wondering as he did so what had happened, so many things, since they had arrived at Taranto. 'I think,' he ventured, 'it's Friday, September 1st, 1939. A day historic.'

Capitaine Le Blanc nodded very solemn in the gallic fashion now. 'Yes, you are correct. It is Friday, the first of September 1939. A day historic.'

'A day historic?' Clarke echoed, using the cavalry captain's strange linguistic construction.

'*Mais oui, un jour historique.*'

'But why?'

The cavalryman looked down at him. 'This morning the Germans attacked Poland. We shall be at war with the Boche within the next forty-eight hours...'

PART TWO

Operation Judgement

ONE

'The Eyeties have gone over the wire!'

The buzz started with one of the stokers down in the engine room. 'Bought something off a gippo bumboat,' he told his mates deep in the heart of the aircraft carrier *Illustrious*. 'Sez he has a cousin – yer know the gippos, they've got cousins every-frigging-where – near the frontier. So the cousin sez the Eyeties went over the wire yesterday. Thousands o' the dago buggers.'

From the boiler room it went to the petty officers' mess. 'You're right, Chiefie,' they said when they heard the buzz, 'it'd just be like old Musso. Waiting till old Jerry saw off our lads in France and then marching into Egypt, where the brown jobs are very bleeding thin on the ground.'

Sub-Lieutenant Gino Green brought it into the wardroom, where the pilots were relaxing after the latest training flight, 'Just heard it from Chiefie Andrews, fellows.' By now the little man's cockney accent had virtually disappeared. Now he had a tendency to say 'orff' and 'old man' at the drop of a hat, something which amused his old friend, George Clarke, greatly. 'The wops have marched. They've crossed the wire into Egypt from Libya... I say, chaps, it looks as if we've got a war on our hands here in the Med. It might not be a big one...'

...'But it's the only war we've got,' the pilots lounging in the battered leather chairs, smoking pipes and reading week-old copies of the London *Times* completed the old saying for him, before someone said in a high pitched excited voice, 'Golly, it looks as if we're going to see some action at last. Ripping good show!'

Lieutenant George Clarke, the senior lieutenant now, frowned. It was nine months or more now since he and Gino had escaped from Libya, to be told by Le Blanc that France and Britain were at war with Germany. In those first few weeks of September all had been hectic chaos. He had been summoned to the new C.-in-C., Admiral 'ABC' Cunningham, and had been ordered to set down everything he could remember about the situation at Taranto forthwith. Together with Gino, soon to be sent home for aircrew training and a commission, they had laboured for forty-eight hours solid making notes, drawings, adding features to the charts that naval intelligence already possessed, pressed all the time by harassed intelligence officers for further details until both of them were exhausted and heartily sick of the whole business.

September had given way to October. Everywhere the Royal Navy was in action, chasing German surface raiders, trying to destroy submarines, escorting convoys with war munitions and equipment across the Atlantic. But on the land nothing happened. The Germans and the Allies remained firmly in their positions, fighting the coldest winter in living memory but that was all. Conflict was limited to 'patrol activity on the Western Front', as the War Office's communiqués had it with boring regularity; and the Italians remained firmly at peace.

But Mussolini was building up a great army in Africa. Under Marshal Graziani, they were said to have as many as 200,000 soldiers on the Libyan frontier with Egypt, known as the 'wire', faced by Major-General O'Connor's 20,000 odd soldiers. Still that Italian Army had not moved all winter. The Italian fleet, too, had remained in its harbours, principally Taranto. 1939 had given way to 1940. The winter ended.

Then suddenly the Germans were attacking, first in Norway, then in the Low Countries. Abruptly the 'phoney war' gave way to a full scale offensive in France. Within six weeks France had been defeated and in the end Italy had come into the war on Germany's side, as Mussolini had always predicted his country would. Now this hot September day, the Italians had finally marched into Egypt and the war had at last come to the Mediterranean.

Now, as all around him the excited young pilots and observers discussed the startling news, Clarke wondered if it was going to be Taranto at last. The new C.-in-C. in the Mediterranean, old 'ABC' as he was always called by the Fleet, had been a destroyer skipper and commander of destroyer flotillas all his career – he had never once been on the staff. He was used to offensive action. Would he take the war to the Italian homeland before the Italian fleet could sail and aid these new operations in Africa?

At midday, just as the officers were assembling in the wardroom drinking a pre-luncheon pink gin, the order came through: 'All officers are to assemble on the flight deck. The C.-in-C. is coming aboard in ten minutes.' There was a sudden cheer. Young faces flushed with excitement, they downed their gins and ran to fetch their caps. Gino, fighting to find his cap, turned to Clarke and cried above the racket the others were making, 'This'll be it, George. I'll bet my bottom dollar on it. It's going to be a wizard party!'

George Clarke allowed himself a little smile, at the 'wizard party' – Gino certainly learned fast – and said, 'Let's wait and see. After all we haven't more than thirty kites in the whole of Egypt for a job like that, and all of them are obsolete. Just let's wait.'

Then they were outside in the glare of the midday sun, watching as the Admiral's brilliant white barge pulled up alongside the *Illustrious*, with the bosuns trilling shrilly on their whistles, as they piped the C.-in-C. aboard.

Admiral Cunningham waited till the captain of the *Illustrious* had reported the officers 'all present and correct', then he ordered them to stand at ease and stared along their ranks, especially at the pilots and the observers drawn up to the left. His keen blue eyes seemed to be etching their faces on his memory, as if it were important to remember them, Clarke thought. He was not an imaginative young man, but he thought he knew why. Before this new conflict in the Med. was over, some of them, perhaps many of them, would be dead, and old 'ABC' wanted to remember them.

'All right, gentlemen,' the Admiral commenced in a voice that carried to the furthest part of the flight deck. 'I know what you're expecting me to tell you this day.' He paused and they tensed with expectation. He smiled slightly, 'Well, I'm not. It's not Taranto. We're not ready for that – *just yet!*'

There was a groan of disappointment from the assembled fliers and 'ABC' nodded his greying head slightly, as if he could understand their disappointment. 'It will come, trust me, it will come in due course. But first things first. We've got to help General O'Connor's chaps in the Western Desert. They're outnumbered ten to one and all his supplies and equipment have to come up long distances from here as you know, whereas Graziani can be supplied from Sicily which is only ninety miles away. So what are we going to do about it?' He answered his own question. 'I shall tell you. In the next forty-eight hours, your aircraft will attack the Italians' three main supply ports of Tripoli, Benghazi and Tobruk in Libya. Harbour installations and

128

any shipping found in those ports will be destroyed. That will, I think, effectively slow down Graziani's advance beyond the wire. *Then*, gentlemen, we shall see what we can do about that other little matter.' He nodded to the ship's captain before saying, 'God speed and good hunting to you all.'

Smartly the skipper of the *Illustrious* stepped forward and shouted, 'Ship's company ... ship's company – *attenshun!*'

The young officers in their starched white shirts and shorts snapped to attention. The captain saluted and the bosuns shrilled their whistles as 'ABC', holding his sword at his side, went down the gangway to the waiting barge. Moments later the excited noisy aircrew were hurrying to the briefing rooms, eager to learn their orders for the coming attack with Gino saying in a slightly bemused manner, his 'posh' accent slipping a little, 'Christ, George, we're going into action at last. What a frigging turn up for the old book!'

The next two days were hectic. As the *Illustrious* steamed up and down the Libyan coast at high speed, launching the 'old stringbags,' as the crews called their antiquated biplanes, on mission after mission. Off they'd go, laden with bombs and torpedoes, keeping a weather eye open for the fast Italian fighters, which could fly a hundred miles an hour faster than they could. Then at low level, braving a sky full of flak – burning balls of high explosive, coming skimming in, their targets looming larger and larger by the second, to release their torpedoes, counting off the seconds as the torpedoes raced through the shallow water towards some freighter or tanker, cheering when they had a 'hit', hurrying to get out leaving behind them death and destruction and huge mushrooms of oil-tinged smoke ascending to the sky.

Meals were grabbed on the run – a cup of tea, perhaps laced with rum, a corned beef sandwich, followed by a few hasty puffs at a 'gasper', before they were hurrying out to the flight deck with new orders and maps, the ground crew, already straining mightily to keep the chocks in place as the old 'stringbags' engines raced and roared. Off again and yet another attack. 'Christ,' as Gino commented, 'right old piecework and Sunday working and no bleeding double time either!'

But like Clarke and the rest he never faltered. They all knew, pilots and observers, that they were buying time for the hard-pressed Army, a couple of brigades of armour, some Indian infantry and a few regular British battalions down there on the ground, fighting and retreating ... pushed ever further back into Egypt by the over-whelming might of the Italians.

On their second day of combat, Clarke and Gino Green struck lucky. They were just approaching Tobruk, noting that the harbour installations were still smoking and burning from the day before, when Gino spotted a small enemy convoy, a couple of coastal freighters and what looked like a small oil tanker, escorted by an Italian destroyer, sleek, new and obviously well armed. 'What d'yer say, George?' Gino asked as purple lights started to flash on the deck of the destroyer and the first flak shells started to explode underneath them.

'Well, we've got a tin fish tucked away under the old stringbag, haven't we? Let's use it.'

'Righto, George,' Gino chortled as Clarke put the Swordfish into a shallow dive, swing-ing the plane from side to side, as the flak shells came curving towards it like glowing golden golf balls. Then suddenly he changed course, directing the plane at the destroyer's midships, ignoring the flak, concentrating on his mission. Now he used the biplane as an aiming device, directing it to fire at the enemy ship which had now abandoned the convoy and was steaming away at a fast lick, making smoke in an attempt to cover its escape.

Clarke grinned, as the plane broke through the smoke screen and the destroyer loomed up right in front of them, her every detail outlined, the smoking cannon, the running sailors, the men already attempting to lower boats, as if they knew what was coming their way. 'Here, Gino, have a last look. I'm going to send that sod to the bottom,' he yelled in triumph. Next instant he pressed the button.

The Swordfish rose twenty feet in the air as the one ton torpedo fell from below her undercarriage. Swiftly Clarke banked to the left, ignoring the flak, while behind him in the observer's seat, Gino counted off the seconds. The 'tin fish' hit the water with a splash. Immediately its engine went into action. It slid through the water, trailing bubbles behind it.

Up above, the Swordfish was buffeted time and time again by shells exploding close to it. The two young officers didn't seem to notice.

Their whole world was dominated by the destroyer, steaming eastwards at thirty knots and the deadly 'tin fish' racing towards her. Suddenly, startlingly, the ship shuddered. It seemed as if she had struck an invisible wall. A tremendous flash. A blast of white smoke. The destroyer's stern rose out of the water, screws thrashing the air impotently. 'By Christ,' Gino yelled exuberantly, 'we've done it … we've hit the sod!'

They had.

With a harsh rending of tearing metal, the destroyer simply broke apart. In an instant men were struggling and thrashing about in the water everywhere, as the steam gushed high in the air, followed an instant later by a great whirring roar as the ship's boilers exploded.

'My God!' Gino Green exclaimed in awe, 'I didn't think war would be like this…'

TWO

'Your captain has recommended you both for the DSC,' old 'ABC' said, looking up at the two young fliers, who still looked tired although they had not flown for the last twenty-four hours. The strain was very obvious on their faces. 'I am going to second his recommendation.'

'Thank you, sir,' Clarke and Green said as one.

'Jolly good show indeed. You and your shipmates have certainly helped to slow down the Italian advance. They're progressing at a snail's pace and I am pleased that the brown jobs,' he smiled at his own use of the Navy's word for soldiers, 'are giving the Italians a bloody nose. Now then, let's get down to business.' Old 'ABC' rose from behind his big desk in the *Warspite* and walked across to the big map of the Mediterranean on the far wall of his cabin. 'I'm planning the attack for Trafalgar Day, October 21st.'

Clarke couldn't restrain himself. 'You

mean, sir, we're going to have a crack at Taranto at last?' he exclaimed.

Old 'ABC' shared his joy. 'Yes, my boy, that we are. I think it will be nice and symbolic to see off the Italian fleet on the anniversary of Nelson's great victory.'

Green looked at his friend and winked. Clarke winked back, tired face full of joy.

'Now then for the last week we've been running reconnaissance flights over Taranto from Malta here. We've been using RAF Sunderland flying boats, which are not really much good for the job and besides the Italians have become used to them coming over and they're waiting for them. So, while we're waiting for the new American Marylands – they're very fast planes indeed – I want some last photographs of the Taranto defences and as you two chaps did the first recce a year ago, I thought I'd give you the honour of doing it this time. What do you say?' He looked at the two young men hard.

'Gosh, sir,' Clarke said enthusiastically, 'I'm sure I can speak for Sub-Lieutenant Green, too … we'd jump at the chance!'

'Good. We've got exactly thirty aircraft for the attack and yours, naturally, will be one of them. So I want you to exercise caution.

Don't take any unnecessary risks. But it is vital that we have the latest information about the enemy's defences.' He tapped the chart at the Bay of Taranto, 'Since they have got used to our reconnaissance planes coming in from the east – from Malta, the Italians have switched most of their ack-ack defence to the east. That doesn't mean to say that they won't have ack-ack to the west – here. But to give you a fighting chance I propose you come in from the west in the hope you can catch them by surprise.' His blue eyes twinkled, 'It isn't every day that you young sprogs are briefed on a mission by an admiral, is it?' 'No sir,' they said as one, returning the old admiral's smile. 'Now to give you an even better chance, the *Illustrious* will carry out another group of sorties against the Libyan ports. Just as you have done before, your comrades and shipmates will attack Tripoli, Tobruk and the like. While they're doing that and the Italians are fully occupied, you will leave the attack force and head due north for Sicily and from there on to Taranto.'

He saw the sudden worried look on their young faces and said hastily, 'I know, I know. It's going to be a tricky business to find the *Illustrious*, as she dodges about all round the Libyan coast, but I'm going to arrange that there will be a twenty-four hour wireless watch for your return and that you are guided as much as possible, without giving away the ship's position to the enemy, back to the carrier. That's the best I can do.'

'Don't worry, sir,' Gino Green said energetically. 'We'll do it and we'll get back with the gen as well!'

'Well spoken, Lieutenant. Now then,' he strode towards them and held out his hand, covered in liver spots which surprised Clarke a little, for he had never thought of 'ABC' as an old man until he remembered the admiral had fought in the Boer War at the turn of the century as a teenager, 'I'm hoping you're going to do me the honour of shaking your hands. I know I'm sending you off on a dangerous task, but I am certain, quite certain, that you will return safely.'

Suddenly the two young men were embarrassed. There were tears in old 'ABC's eyes.

It was night, but a full moon blazed, illuminating the sea in a silver-white light, as the dispatcher flashed his signals at the waiting planes, their engines roaring as they readied for take-off. Number One raced along the flight deck, as the great carrier surged through the water off the enemy coast. When it seemed it must inevitably go over the side and fall into the sea, the pilot jerked back the stick and the 'stringbag' was airborne. Now plane after plane followed, each breaking to left and right as they left the carrier.

As Number Six, Clarke gave the old plane full throttle, taking pleasure in the sweet note of the engine. It was functioning perfectly. The dispatcher flashed his light. 'Hold on to your hat, Gino,' Clarke yelled over the intercom, 'here we go!'

'All aboard for the Skylark,' Gino yelled back.

Then they were rolling, rushing across the flight deck. Ahead, the bows loomed up. There were only yards to go. In a minute they'd be over the side. Clarke jerked back the stick. The 'stringbag' answered immediately. The plane rose, cleared the bow and then they were gaining height rapidly. Clarke gave a little sigh, as he always did on take-off. As a young pilot he had ditched twice and he hadn't liked the sensation. He was always glad when he managed to clear the flight deck successfully on take-off.

Now he concentrated on getting out of the way of the rest of the squadron as they formed and prepared to attack the Italian installations. Dimly he could see the fires caused by the other squadron and he told himself his shipmates would be in for a hot reception. The Italians would be waiting for them now. Then he forgot the rest of the squadron as he concentrated on the task in hand and turned the plane on a northerly course.

Time passed leadenly. At a steady 100 m.p.h. the 'stringbag' beat northwards. To their front they spotted the red glare of Mount Etna and Clark said through the intercom, 'Sicily, we'll steer clear of the island, Gino.'

Gino knew why. There were plenty of Italian air bases on the island. It was better not to alert them.

Altering course a little, flashing glances at the angry glare of the volcano, Clarke steered a north-easterly course and began to head for the mainland.

Reggio di Calabria loomed up out of the silver darkness.

'The Eyeties' blackout's not much cop,' Gino commented, looking over the side at the blaze of lights. 'Perhaps they're scared of the dark.'

'Well, they're obviously not scared of us,'

Clarke answered. 'I'm told the Italians turn off the lights when a plane approaches. They don't take the blackout as seriously as we do. Let's hope it's the same at Taranto.'

He lapsed into silence and started to follow the coastline with the aid of the clearly lit, little coastal towns. Now they were approaching the places where they had fled the previous year in what seemed now another lifetime. How much had changed since! Their old ship the *Glorious* had been sunk off Norway, taking with her so many of his friends and former shipmates. Back home his house had been bombed and destroyed in one of the German raids on Plymouth. His mother was working again, too, on a farm in remotest Yorkshire as probably the oldest land girl in the kingdom. Yes, things had changed and he had changed with them. He was no longer that callow, green youth with that naïve sense of decency and honour which Dartmouth had knocked into him. Now he was determined to kill, in whatever way was necessary, however brutally, as long as he, his shipmates, and, ultimately, the country survived.

Off Rossano, he turned the plane to the sea in order to cross the Bay of Taranto.

Behind him Gino stared routinely to left

and right on the watch for enemy night fighters, for he reasoned that of all the Italian coastal cities, the one most likely to be protected from the air would be Taranto.

The minutes passed. Now they were slowly approaching the other side of the Gulf of Taranto. In the distance Clarke could just make out the pinpoints of light which were lighthouses guiding the shipping along the coast. The full moon still shone, too, bathing the sea below a bright silver. All the light was good, he told himself, but also bad. He wouldn't have to light up the harbour to do his reconnaissance. At the same time, it meant the old 'stringbag' could be detected more easily. He sniffed and told himself he'd worry about that when he was over the target.

Now he could see the curve of the inner harbour at Taranto. Just as at Reggio, there was no blackout, which told him that so far their plane had not been detected. He started to take the plane up. He'd try two runs: one at high level and the other at low. At high level, the patently simple device, which had just been invented and which was still highly secret, of using the heat from the engine to stop the camera's lens from steaming up at high altitude, would allow him to fly over the target without too much danger from prowling night fighters. Then to be absolutely sure he was getting the pictures that old 'ABC' wanted, he'd go in at that dangerous low level. In, fast and furious and then out.

Swiftly he explained his plan to Gino and told him of the dangers, which left the other man apparently unconcerned. 'Up to you, George,' he said easily, 'you're the skipper.'

They came out of the high-level fly-over without any trouble. Below the lights still blazed, indicating that the Italian radio detection beam hadn't yet picked them up. Now Clarke prepared for the low-level sortie. 'All right, Gino,' he said, 'here we go.' He started to bring the old biplane down, knowing that he wouldn't get away with it this time. The Italians might even get a visual contact for all he knew; the moonlight was strong enough.

The 'stringbag' flew lower and lower. Now Clarke was flying at perhaps one thousand feet. He had decided not to take 'ABC's advice. He would come over the land. The Italians had been used to the reconnaissance planes zooming in from the sea; he would do it differently.

They came closer. Suddenly whole sections of the city went black. They had been spotted! 'That's torn it!' Gino yelled. Clarke ignored the remark. Instead he concentrated on his task. Now the port was totally blacked out. But he could still see the silver sheen of the two inner harbours by the light of the moon. Still he was going to make quite sure that his photographs had absolutely clear definition. He pressed the flare release, knowing as he did so that he was increasing the danger to the plane.

The first flare exploded, illuminating the port in its harsh silver light. Gino started the cameras. Down below a scarlet light winked abruptly. *Flak!*

Brown puffballs began to explode about them. The old plane was rocked violently from side to side, as if punched by a gigantic fist. Grimly Clarke stuck to his course. He soared over the causeway where Irma had once had her 'establishment'. Down below, outlined starkly by the eerie glowing silver light, he could see the grey outlines of the Italian battleships at anchor, with beyond, the sleeker outlines of the destroyers and submarines. He wet his suddenly parched lips. What a tempting target they made! There were scores of them.

'Hit this place, George,' Gino yelled glee-

143

fully over the intercom, 'and it's ta-ta to the Eyetie fleet!'

Clarke didn't answer. He was busy. He kept the plane on an even keel as more and more shells started to explode all about them. Searchlights were flicking on too, searching the heavens, trying to cone on the lone intruder so that the guns could shoot it out of the sky.

To the right, a quick-firer started to pump glowing, red-hot shells at the biplane. They came up in a solid wall. It was like flying through a mass of molten steel. Clarke gasped. Would they make it? They did. With a gasp of relief this time, he swung the plane to starboard and then soared upwards, leaving the flak falling behind him. But he knew that he wasn't out of the mess yet. He knew the Italians would be scrambling their fast Fiat 50s and Macchis to seek and destroy the intruder, planes that had the advantage over the antiquated Swordfish. Now he had to make a decision, an overwhelming one: should he fly high or at sea-level? 'What do you think, Gino?' he rasped swiftly. 'High or low?'

'Low, sir,' Gino responded. 'Sorry, low George.'

Clarke grinned despite the seriousness of

144

the situation. Gino still couldn't forget what they had once been, the last time they had visited Taranto. 'At least if we have to ditch it low we've got a chance.'

'Right, low it is.' Swiftly Clarke brought the plane down.

Now they were scurrying over the Bay of Taranto at not more than a hundred feet, radial engine going all out, the prop thrashing the waves into a milky fury. Behind them the guns ceased firing one by one and Clark knew the Italian flak gunners had been alerted by their air force people. The night fighters had scrambled. They had been ordered to stop firing so that they didn't shoot down their own people.

He opened the throttle, giving the plane full power. He started to shake and tremble under the impact. But Clarke had no fears on that score. The Swordfish was a tough old bird. It could stand a lot of punishment, he knew. Little did George Clarke know just how soon the old 'stringbag' would need to stand a great deal of punishment – and then some...

THREE

The Macchi caught up with them, as they had just finished crossing the Gulf of Taranto. Suddenly, it flashed out of the silver darkness, machine guns chattering frighteningly, bullets hissing in a bright red stream just above the cockpit.

Clarke reacted instinctively. He yawed to one side and then dived steeply. The tactic put the Italian pilot off – for a moment. He soared by them and, for an instant, disappeared out of sight. In a flash he had recovered and came in for another sortie, guns blazing. Gino sprang to the plane's single machine gun. 'Try this on for size, Eyetie bastard,' he yelled angrily and pressed the trigger. A stream of white tracer headed straight for the Macchi. Again the Italian pilot was put off his stroke. He broke to the right in the same instant that Clarke took the old 'stringbag' right down to the water.

Now he was skimming over the surface of the sea at perhaps twenty feet. It was a terribly risky tactic, especially in darkness when it was so hard to judge distances. One wrong move and they'd be in the water. Clarke knew that. But it was the only defensive tactic he could think of. The Italian pilot would know, too, the risks involved in coming so low. Perhaps that would deter him.

Clarke guessed wrong. The Italian was skilled and obviously fearless, as well. He dropped out of the sky like a stone and took up the chase once more, sticking doggedly to Clarke's tail, squeezing off short, sharp bursts as Clarke weaved desperately from side to side.

By now he was lathered in sweat as he managed to escape death and destruction with just seconds to spare. Behind him Gino hammered away frantically with his own gun, hopelessly outclassed by the much faster Italian fighter with its four machine guns. Instinctively Clarke knew their luck wouldn't hold much longer. Still at the back of his mind was the desperate hope that he would pull it off and bring those greatly needed photographs back to the *Illustrious*.

Now the Macchi was only two hundred feet behind its quarry. Gino, sweating and cursing furiously, could see the Italian plane quite clearly. Yet the Italian pilot seemed invulnerable. Every time he dodged the bursts of fire which Gino directed towards him expertly. Suddenly Gino realised that the other man hadn't closed with the 'string-bag' altogether because he was scared of their single machine gun. Why else did he not close to finish the Swordfish off once and for all?

'George,' he yelled urgently into the intercom, 'I'm going to try to fool the bastard. You're on your own for half a mo.'

'What...'

Clarke's frantic words were drowned by another burst of machine gun fire.

Gino slumped forward as if dead or seriously wounded, jerking the machine gun upwards. The Italian pilot seized his chance. He surged forward, closing the gap between the two planes rapidly so that this time he wouldn't miss. In a flash he was just one hundred feet behind the Swordfish. Gino, faking death, could see his face quite clearly in the green glow coming from his instrument panel. In one instant he'd fire and that would be that. Gino beat him to it. He jerked the machine gun down and pressed the trigger hard. Slugs poured out of the muzzle of the gun. Bits of metal started to fall off the Macchi. White glycol spurted up from the ruptured engine. *'I've got the sod,'* Gino yelled crazily, but at the same moment a burst of fire ripped the length of the fuselage. In the pilot's seat Clarke yelped with pain. He had been hit in the leg. It felt as if someone had just thrust a red-hot poker into his right thigh. Immediately he felt sick and fuggy with pain.

Behind them the Macchi fell out of the sky. It hit the water with a tremendous splash and went right under, carried to the bottom of the Gulf by its own speed and weight.

Gino slumped back in his seat, all energy spent. It was as if a tap had been opened somewhere and everything had drained out of his body, leaving him weak and ener-vated. But he was startled into renewed activity by Clarke's voice over the intercom, saying, 'Gino, I've been hit. I don't know how bad. But I feel a bit faint. I'm going to take her up four or five hundred feet and keep close to the coast. Strap on your chute, just in case.'

Gino rallied at once, 'You'll make it George. We're not going into the bag with the Eyeties. We've been there once and we didn't like it. Remember? Now then, George, home and don't spare the horses.'

How he managed the flight back, Clarke

never remembered afterwards. Everything was a pain-racked blue. Once he passed out, but somehow he managed to keep control and the plane on a steady course. In the meantime Gino, behind him, did his best to keep him going. He told dirty jokes, stories of his sexual experiences in red light districts in ports all over the world and he sang bawdy songs, all the while urging, 'It won't be long now, George. The old *Illustrious* won't let us down, mark my words...'

'Tight as a drum, never been done, queen of all the fairies...' Gino was singing lustily, as the wireless started to crackle up front, *'O what a pity she's only one titty to feed the baby with... Poor little bugger's got only one udder...'*

'I've got a fix on the *Illustrious*,' Clarke blurted out, voice thick with relief. 'We can't be very far off her ... the signals are very strong.'

'Whacko!' Gino chortled happily. 'I knew you'd do it, George. Can't keep a good man down.' Joyfully he launched into *'Up came a spider, sat down beside her, whipped his old bazooka out and this is what he said ... get hold of this, bash-bash...'*

Ten minutes later, weak and feeling faint, Clarke spotted the first flare from the big carrier. He breathed a sigh of relief. He knew he was pretty badly wounded, his trouser leg was soaked in blood. Now the medics could look after him.

He came lower, peering through a red haze. There she was. Steaming on a steady course, doing perhaps twenty knots, clearly outlined in the silver light of the waning moon. The ship had already turned into the wind to facilitate his landing. Now the skipper ordered the deck and pillar lights switched on to aid the 'stringbag' further and, by straining his eyes, Clarke could see the illuminated paddles of the 'batman' who would supervise the landing.

He reduced speed and came lower still. Behind him Gino said a hurried prayer. Landing on a carrier was difficult enough at any time. Now they were landing at night with a wounded pilot at the controls. It wasn't going to be easy, he knew that all right.

'Hold tight,' Clarke said weakly over the intercom, 'here we go, Gino.' He raised the Swordfish's nose slightly to help reduce speed even more and started to level her up with the flight deck. He was almost down now. Suddenly his head began to swim, a red mist threatened to engulf him yet again. He felt he was going to faint. With an effort of sheer, naked will power he pulled himself together just in time to see the batman wagging his illuminated paddles furiously. 'You're coming in at an angle, George,' Gino yelled urgently.

At the very last moment, Clarke managed to jerk back the stick. The fabric protesting violently, the biplane swept over the deck and upwards, as Clarke tried to overcome his shock. He had nearly written the kite off.

He circled the *Illustrious* and came in for another go, biting his bottom lip till the blood came in an attempt to use the pain to make him stay alert. Again he began to feel faint. Doggedly he pulled himself together and went through the landing procedures. He levelled the plane with the flight deck, reduced speed, lifted the nose to brake his speed even further and then he was coming down, his head whirling and spinning, bitter bile welling up in his throat as if he might vomit at any moment.

The tyres hit the deck. He heard the screech of rubber. He was rolling forward, but too fast. Down went the flaps. Still he was moving too fast. On the deck the ratings scattered and the fire-dowsers started putting on their fire-fighting helmets. In his daze Clarke saw them. He turned off the petrol supply. Then, in the same moment that the Swordfish hit the arrester wire and was brought to a bone-shaking stop, his head slammed against the controls and everything went black.

Gino freed himself frantically from his harness. Ratings were rushing towards them. Someone was squirting foam. He scrambled forward to Clarke's cockpit and gasped. The floor was full of sticky congealing blood. He put his arms underneath the unconscious pilot's arms and heaved. Ratings were jumping on the wing to help. 'Gently does it ... gently, lads,' he ordered.

They got him out and laid him on the deck of the carrier. A surgeon commander, still in his underpants, came running up. He acted promptly. He pumped a syringe into the unconscious man's arm and then with amazing speed, he bound a tourniquet above the wounded leg, crying, 'Stretcher-bearers ... come on you stretcher bearers, let's get this officer to the sick bay, *at the double!*'

Two hours later, just after he had been down to the sick bay for the second time to view an unconscious and very ashen-faced George, Gino was summoned to the captain's office. Hanging from pegs on wires running back and forth across it were their wet photographs, dripping like a house-wife's Monday washing line.

The captain took off his horn-rimmed spectacles and beamed at him. 'Excellent show, Green,' he barked. 'We've got every-thing we want. The battle wagons, the dock installations, the ack-ack, the blooming lot. Fine job of work.'

'Thank you, sir,' Green answered, thinking that only a year ago, he had never even spoken to a Royal Navy ship's captain. He was coming up in the world. His dad and mum would be proud of him.

Although it was barely dawn, the captain indicated the bottle on the opposite table. 'Help yourself to a pink gin if you wish and a gasper. Must have been one hell of a night for the two of you. How's Lieutenant Clarke?'

As if he'd been accustomed to this way of living all his life, Gino Green poured himself a stiff pink gin and took a hand-rolled cigarette from the ornate silver box. 'The surgeon-commander has got the bullet out. He's lost a lot of blood. But there are no complications. The surgeon commander says he has to go into dock, though, sir, when we arrive back at Alex.'

'Of course, of course. I've just received a signal from the C.-in-C. We've been ordered back to port.' He looked knowingly at the little cockney. 'The op.'s naturally on now that we've got all this stuff,' he indicated the photographs.

'Sir,' Gino ventured, dragging at the cigarette which had been specially made for the captain in an exclusive little shop in Bond Street, 'I wonder if I can ask a favour?'

'Fire away, Green,' the skipper said airily.

'Sir, I've always flown with Lieutenant Clarke. I don't really fancy flying with anyone else until he's better. The surgeon-commander says he'll need about a week to ten days in hospital before he's fit for light duties. So I wonder if I could have ten days' leave to keep an eye on him until he's back on his feet again.'

The captain's eyes twinkled. 'You're like a bloody mother hen, Green. Of course you can. Normally I wouldn't give any one of the ship's crew a special leave at this stage of the show, but we've got ten days before the op. starts. And you've done more than your share so far in this war. Yes, tell the Number One to mark you down for ten days' special leave in Alex, once we get there.'

'Thank you, sir, thank you very much.' Gino drained the rest of his pink gin hurriedly, as if he half-expected the skipper to change his mind, picked up his cap, clicked to attention. 'I'll be off, sir. Thank you for the cigarette and the drink.'

The captain waved his hand in dismissal. 'Now go and get your head down, my boy. Good morning.'

But Gino Green did not go straight to his cabin. Instead he went up on the lift to the flight deck. Mechanics were hustling about, folding the wings of returning swordfish aircraft and sending them down below in the lifts. Others were clearing up the rest of the mess made by their own 'stringbags'. All was haste and hard work, carried out under the watchful eyes of the ack-ack gunners seated at their 'Chicago pianos', great banks of heavy machine guns, and the quick-firing Bofors.

Gino yawned, watching the new sun slip over the horizon, colouring the sea a blood-red hue. He had seen the same scene many times before, but it always impressed him; so many men working together for a common cause on a ship which for many of them was more of a home to them than their real one. Instinctively he knew, with the sudden one hundred percent clarity of a vision, that not many of these men would survive the war. The odds were against it: one lone aircraft carrier in the Med. against the mighty Italian Air Force with its hundreds, thousands, of planes. In the end the *Illustrious* was bound to be sunk. Perhaps he'd get the chop himself.

But at that moment he was happy, really happy, a young man in his prime, fighting fit, with a new gong and ten days' leave in Alex in front of him. 'Lovely grub,' he said in the accent of the old East End. *'Lovely grub.'* Then he went back to the lift, telling himself there might well be 'pusser's' bangers and kidneys, with a bit of luck, for breakfast...

FOUR

Alex was in a hell of a flap, Gino could see that. As he drove in the ancient taxi to his hotel, he could see the palm-lined avenues filled with khaki-clad soldiers, rifles slung over their shoulders, hair bleached to tow, 'browned-off', angry with the heat, the conditions, the 'Gippos'. Their every gesture seemed to reveal their anger, their boredom and fear. For soon they knew they would be going 'up the blue' – into the Western Desert – and would meet what was waiting for them there.

For the Italians had reached Sidi Barrani now and had paused there, while they waited for further petrol and supplies and everyone knew, or thought they did, that O'Connors' tiny army and handful of tanks could not stop the massive Italian juggernaut, once it started moving again, which it would soon.

Once, when his taxi was stopped by an Egyptian policeman wearing a red fez, Gino saw a young, angry-faced soldier knock away a basket of dates proffered by an Egyptian hawker, with an angry, 'Sod off, you Gippo wog.' Then the soldier stamped on a bunch of dates before moving on. Then the hawker spat after him and directed a stream of angry Arabic invective at his khaki-clad back.

'What did he say?' Gino asked the driver as the taxi started to move again.

The native driver grinned, showing a set of gleaming gold teeth. 'Why, Effendi, soon you'll be running for the Nile, you English dog.'

Gino grinned. The Gippo had a sense of humour, at least.

Over lunch in the hotel which had been taken over by the military, eating corned beef fritters and tasteless dehydrated mashed potatoes, the chatter of the staff wallahs was all about those who had already fled the great port and those who would do so soon. They were the rich Egyptians who had supplied the British Army for years and the countless British civilians who had what the staff wallahs called a 'cushy number', the various wives and mistresses of high ranking officers who had infringed regulations to join their menfolk, now all of them fought to get on the one train a day which left for Palestine, jeered at and insulted by the native porters who would point overhead at the port's scavengers, the bronze-brown kites, and sneer, 'They'll be waiting for you when the air raids start.'

But not all the important Egyptians had fled, Gino heard. Many were waiting for Italians to come and 'free' them. Even the gross young King of Egypt, usually concerned only with his nubile teenage mistresses and pornographic photographers, had summoned up enough interest in the war to go to the British Minister in Cairo and tell him, 'When the war's over, for God's sake put down the white man's burden and go.' Obviously, the staff officers, chatting so bitterly all around Gino thought the King wouldn't have long to wait before the British put down the 'white man's burden' and went.

Gino gave up on the food and the company in the end. The grub was rotten, he told himself moodily, and the people weren't much better. There was a stink of defeatism in the air. These people, soldiers and civilians, had no faith in a British victory. Didn't they know the Navy had been fighting – and winning – from the very first day the Eyeties had entered the war? Naturally they couldn't have known the Med. Fleet was planning a great strike which would knock out most of the Eyetie Navy for good. But couldn't they have faith?

For a while he sat in the shade of his balcony watching the afternoon scene below. In the stifling heat Levantine merchants sat in their flowered pyjamas, fanning themselves and sweating heavily. Little boys were stringing flowers into necklaces and trying to sell them to the women drivers of British Army trucks. Black men, once slaves, were shovelling masses of cold white beans down their throats greedily.

But as the heat started to wane, he decided it was time to go and visit George in hospital. Strangely enough he felt, *he* would be cheered up by the visit, rather than George.

George Clarke was pale, but obviously recovering. He lay in a long cool ward of injured officers, some sleeping, some reading and smoking, his wounded leg heavily bandaged and propped up by a little wooden stand. Nurses in starched white uniforms came and went, bearing trays of medicines or with bedpans discreetly covered by immaculate white cloths.

The sight cheered Gino up immediately. There was order, efficiency and purpose about the place despite the wounded men. These men had actually shed their blood for their country in battle, but there seemed none of the moaning and griping that he had found back in the hotel. 'Anything you want, George?' he asked, seating himself on the little chair next to George's bed.

George shook his head. 'No, they do pretty well for us in here.' He grinned, his face still very white but powerful all the same, 'But I bet *you* want something.'

Gino shared his grin, 'Come to think of it,

I could do with a bit of the other. It's been a long time.'

'But don't catch anything,' George cautioned him and lowering his voice said, 'I want you with me when we go – well, you know.' He looked anxiously from side to side to see if anyone was listening. No one was.

'Do you think you'll be out by then? Trafalgar Day isn't far off,' Gino said.

'I'll be out, even if I go out on crutches,' George said, his face very determined. 'Do you think I'd miss a party like that? It'll be one of the biggest of the whole war, as far as the Navy's concerned. Now then don't waste any more time on an old cripple like me,' he flashed Gino a smile. 'Go and enjoy yourself. And remember,' he wagged a warning finger at the other man. 'Don't do anything I wouldn't do.'

'All right, George, I'll be in to see you tomorrow.' He winked as a very pretty nurse went by carrying a bedpan. 'You might even get lucky with that one.'

'Not with that old battle-axe of a matron in charge. Gosh, she'd have you court-martialled for just *looking* at one of her girls, never mind touching 'em.'

Half an hour later, Gino was strolling in

the shade in one of the inner city's big squares. As usual there were touts everywhere, some only boys, all appraising the virtues of their 'ladies'. 'All pink inside, sir… Just like white ladies … very clean … very cheap.'

Time and time again Gino shooed them away. He couldn't face any raddled old Gippo whore. He'd had enough of them when he'd still been on the lower deck and couldn't afford anything better. Now he had a pocket full of pay and wanted to treat himself to something white, or near white. There were always plenty of classy French whores in Alex. He just had to find the pimp who'd take him to the right knocking shop…

The pimp was short and dark and not Egyptian, though Gino couldn't make out from his accent when he spoke in English what nationality he was. He opened with the standard ploy, 'You want woman, sir? Very pretty.' He rolled his eyes, 'knows lots of good tricks. Anything sir wants.'

'White?'

The pimp looked at him in feigned indignation. 'Yessir. Naturally, sir.'

'How much?' Gino's old cockney sense of the value of money came to the surface.

'In English pounds – ten.' He held up his outstretched fingers to make the sum quite clear. 'Sovereigns are better, sir.' He looked shrewdly at Gino.

Gino knew why. Like all the businessfolk in Alex now, the pimp preferred not to hold British currency. They thought it would be worthless when the Eyeties came. Again he was angered by the defeatism of the locals. But the urge in his loins was too strong now. He *needed* a woman. 'All right,' he snapped curtly. 'Take me to her. Let the dog see the bone.'

Five minutes later the pimp was leading him into a cool dark house away from one of the main squares. It smelled a little stale, as if it had not been properly aired for a long time and there were damp stains on the peeling wallpaper. Still it had once belonged to some rich Levantine or other. There were cracked, faded oils of oriental beauties on the wall, all breast and behind, and there was a lot of chipped gilt on the ceiling which was decorated with more naked females carved in wood and plaster.

The pimp clapped his hands. A side door opened immediately. Two women were standing there, dark and pretty, perhaps in their thirties, and dressed in bright silk dresses which revealed their generous figures all too well.

Gino licked his lips. They were a bit old, but by the look of them, they knew their stuff. Which one was he going to take? The darker of the two women attempted to make the decision for him. 'One for ten, two for twenty.' Like the pimp she held up her beringed plump fingers, painted a bright red, as if they had been dipped in blood.

'For all night?' he asked, wondering at the woman's accent. It didn't seem particularly French to him, but then Gino considered, he didn't speak more than half a dozen words of French.

She shook her head in the Egyptian way. 'No, for one hour.' Again the finger illustrated the number.

He laughed. 'Give me two hours – I need that to get into my stride. Then it's twenty quid.'

She considered gravely. Finally she nodded, 'Two hours, it shall be.' Minutes later he was upstairs lying naked on a very large bed that smelled of cheap scent, oriental tobacco and ancient lecheries and watched as they undressed each other. It was a true and tried performance; they had obviously done it many times before; all the same it excited Gino.

The taller of the two came round the back of the other, kissing the nape of her neck and darting feathery little kisses at her ears and plump shoulders. Slowly, very slowly, she released the little whore's bra and let her breasts fall. They were plump and big and dark. That done, the whore bent slightly and fixed her mouth to the topless whore's left nipple. She sucked it wetly while the smaller one threw back her head, eyes screwed close, moaning as if she were in the throes of unbearable passion, which perhaps she was.

The dressed whore sank to her knees, trailing a line of kisses down the other's stomach until she reached her panties. Delicately, bloodred fingers hooked, as if she were soon to reveal a thing of indescribable beauty, she picked at the elastic. She paused and stared back at him as if to ensure that he was enjoying himself. Gino was. She could see that quite obviously.

Teasingly, slowly, she began to draw down the silk of the black knickers. 'There,' she breathed and planted a kiss on the other whore's naked abdomen, making sure not to hide the fact that her vagina was shaven and powdered like that of a child. 'You like?' she sighed.

'I like,' he agreed, not recognising his own voice. 'Christ,' he told himself, 'Heaven help a sailor on a night like this!'

Now it was the bigger whore's turn. She played coy and reluctant and the smaller whore slapped her lightly across the face when she refused to reveal her breasts when she had removed her bra. With a grunt of feigned anger, she pulled the woman's arms back to display enormous breasts with large dark-brown nipples. 'Oh my Gawd,' Gino moaned. 'You could get yer head in between that pair and not hear a thing for a month or two!'

Her panties followed. Again the smaller one seemed to have to use force, ripping them down. *'Open,'* she commanded and slapped the woman's plump buttocks, *'Quick!'* She inserted a finger in between the other woman's legs – hard. She squirmed.

Gino squirmed too. It was all getting too much for him. 'Ladies,' he moaned, 'Better get to bed quick. Otherwise I think there's going to be a major accident...'

FIVE

'Aviatore di marine ... sa qualche cosa,' lying on the bed next to the naked whore who was snoring softly, Gino took in the words very vaguely.

He was exhausted. The two whores had worked him over very professionally. It was 'once round the world' and then back again in a most delightful manner. They had had no inhibitions and as he remarked gleefully after the first bout, 'You girls really dance a smashing mattress polka... I can see you like your work!'

Now, just barely awake, he listened to the words idly until it suddenly dawned on him that they were in Italian. *'Italian!'* a harsh little voice at the back of his mind rasped, *'they're not French; they're Eyeties!'*

Abruptly he was wide awake and very alert. He peered through his almost closed eyelids, trying not to reveal that he was awake. The pimp was standing at the open door of the bedroom. Opposite him, naked save for a pair of black silk knickers, the

168

other whore was holding up his uniform jacket, pointing to the wings above the gold stripe of the sleeve. 'He's an aviator,' she had just said, 'he'll know something.'

Expertly, as though he had done this often enough before, the little pimp went through the pockets, taking out his wallet, examining his officer's card and its other contents. Finally he shook his head and handed the jacket back to the whore in the black knickers, *'niente'*, he said, 'nothing.'

An hour later an excited Gino was in the Office of Naval Intelligence telling his story to a keen-eyed lieutenant-commander, who didn't say a word until Gino had finished, though he did smile a little roguishly when Gino mentioned the two women. 'Italian,' he mused, sitting back in his chair, while Gino took a grateful sip of his ice-cold Rheingold beer. 'There's always been a small Italian community in Alex. Most of them are perfectly harmless and law-abiding. As soon as Italy entered the war we arrested those we suspected of having contacts with the enemy, obviously we didn't nab all of them.' He looked straight at Gino, keen eyes searching the other man's face. 'What do *you* think they were after?'

'Well, sir, they seemed very interested in the fact that I was a flier and not just another naval officer. Therefore, my guess, is that they are after something on our air operational side.'

'Exactly, my thinking too. And the only major air operation that we are going to undertake soon is the one you know about.'

'Yes, sir. That's it.' Gino agreed.

'And you know, too, that if the Italians become aware of our plans in advance, there would be slaughter. They'd mass their Air Force around Taranto – hundreds of them – and your handful of "stringbags" wouldn't stand a chance.'

Gino nodded grimly. 'Yes, that's the way it would be, sir,' he said sombrely. 'There are no two ways about it.'

The lieutenant-commander stared out of the window. Now the heat of the day was over, a group of defaulters were being drilled by a tough-looking petty officer with a pacing stick under his arm, marching the bare-headed matelots back and forth over the parade ground, barking orders at them, harassing them, warning them to 'open them legs. Nothing'll fall out. Now bags o' swank! Remember you're in the Royal Navy not the Gippo Navy. *Left … right … left…*'

The other officer spoke again. 'First things first,' he said. 'We'll arrest your pimp and the two ladies of the night. We'll grill 'em and find out what they know. If we do find out that they know something about the Trafalgar Day op., I'm afraid I'll have to inform the C.-in-C. Then it'll be up to him.'

Gino looked at him dismayed. 'Not that ... not after that bloody work.' For a moment he reverted to his old cockney accent and the lieutenant-commander looked slightly surprised at the change in the speech pattern.

'Well, let's hope that won't be necessary. Now then,' he reached in his drawer and fetched out a pistol, 'we'll go in when its well dark. Tennish. Then they'll be in – er – business and hopefully we'll catch them on the hop.' He grinned briefly at Gino. 'Want to come along for the ride?'

'You betcha, sir.'

'Good, then go and find yourself a popgun while I organise a raiding party, a good half dozen leading ratings and petty officers. Off you go.'

Gino went...

The noise of the great port was muted now. Here and there a horse-drawn gharry went by, its string of bells jingling prettily, but most of the natives had vanished and the old house itself was silent.

Carefully they moved across the parched lawn under the palm trees, each man carrying a pick handle with the petty officer in charge of the raiding party cradling a wicked-looking tommy-gun in his arms.

Lieutenant-Commander Davidson, the Intelligence officer, revolver in hand, signalled left and right. Under the command of the petty officer, half the ratings went round towards the back of the house. Davidson was taking no chances. He nodded to Gino and the latter drew his revolver too. As silently as they could they ascended the stone steps leading up to the house. Now they could hear muted laughter coming from inside the tightly shuttered house. There was the clink of glasses too.

Davidson sniffed. 'Looks as if your lady friends have got more visitors. Busy little bees,' he whispered.

'If you'll pardon my French, sir, I bet that couple have had more fucks than they've had hot dinners.'

Davidson smiled in the yellow light coming from the street lamp outside. Gingerly he started to turn the door handle, while

172

behind him the ratings tensed. It opened without a squeak. Ahead the passage was empty and dimly lit. 'You two stand watch here,' Davidson ordered.

The two ratings selected nodded and held their pick handles more firmly in their brawny paws.

'Come on.'

Systematically they opened the doors of the downstairs' rooms and peered inside. They were all deserted. But now they could hear laughter and the clink of glasses more clearly. 'Upstairs, sir,' Gino suggested in a whisper.

'You're right.'

Hardly daring to breathe, the little party started to climb the stairs. Now they could hear the sounds quite clearly. It was the whores all right and someone speaking English in what Gino told himself was a 'toffee-nosed accent'.

Davidson flashed a last glance around his little party and then with his hand on the doorknob, shrilled three blasts on his whistle, his signal to those around the back. The next moment he had burst through the door, crying, 'Hands up everyone...'

He gasped. A naked man lay on the bed, dressed in black stockings and a garter belt, while the two naked whores fondled him, 'Oh my God,' Davidson exclaimed, 'it's old Carruthers!'

At his side Gino grinned. The officer, for he took him to be an officer, was old and paunchy and he looked an absolute idiot in the silk stockings. Now he sat up and said, his voice a mixture of anger and helplessness, 'I say, Davidson, bit much bursting in on a chap like this… I hope it won't get out, will it?'

By way of an answer, Davidson jerked his revolver at the three on the bed and rasped, 'Get dressed, please, quickly.' He turned to Gino. 'There's one missing, isn't there?'

'Yes, that little squirt of a pimp. Got to find him. The whores are just his workers. Probably uses them to pick up chaps, officers, like our unhappy friend over there.' He indicted the fat officer who had turned his back to the grinning ratings as he undid his suspender belt to take off his black stockings.

Davidson grinned and, putting his hand in front of his mouth, he whispered, 'Might interest you to know, Lieutenant, that our friend is a full captain on old 'ABC's staff.'

'Phew!'

'All right,' Davidson was businesslike

again, 'Let's find him if he's here.'

Gino asked the whores in fluent Italian. Their mouths dropped open in surprise and one of them cried, *'Porco Madonna, e Italiano!'*

'Yes, now get on with it,' Gino snapped.

The bigger one shrugged and said, 'Carlo–'

Her words were drowned by the sudden crack of a pistol, followed an instant later by the angry chatter of a tommy-gun. 'That's him,' Davidson cried, 'Come on. You two, watch those women!' Together he and Gino raced out into the corridor again and towards the back of the house. From outside they could already hear feeble moaning and the cries of the petty officer's party, as the PO cried, 'Watch the sod. Tricky lot, yon Eyeties, lads.'

They found the little pimp outside on the grass with the petty officer glowering down at him fiercely, tommy-gun at the ready. 'Tried to do a bunk, sir. When he spotted us, he pulled a gun on us.' He shrugged. 'His aim was none too good.'

Davidson bent over the pimp on one knee and shone his torch on him. His eyes were closed and he was writhing and trembling with pain, words pouring from his mouth, as

175

if as long as he talked he would live. 'Goner, I should imagine. But we'll try to do our best for him. What's that lingo he's talking? Italian as well?'

'Yes sir, he's saying a prayer and asking the Holy Mother of God to save him.'

Davidson shrugged. 'Afraid it looks to me as if he's out of luck. Come on, let's get to the phone inside and ring for a naval ambulance. We don't want him to go to the Gippo hospital. They'd finish him off in five minutes flat. No, on second thoughts, Green, you stay with him. He might say something we can use.'

'Yes, sir.' Green knelt down. Then, as if from some long-forgotten instinct, he searched the dying man's pockets and found what he had expected to find, a rosary. He folded it and pressed it into the Italian's hands. Weakly the pimp opened his eyes momentarily and whispered, *'grazie.'*

The Italian pimp died just after dawn. The naval doctors had tried to pull him around, but had failed. All the time Gino stood near the operating table or by his bed in the hope of catching something the dying man might say. In vain. Once he started shouting out orders, as if he were used to giving them and having them obeyed. Gino concluded that he had served as an officer at one time and had volunteered or had been seconded to the intelligence-gathering branch. At six thirty that morning he had sat up in bed suddenly, eyes wide open, and, raising his right arm quite firmly, had cried in a loud voice, '*Il Duce*' before falling backwards, dead.

Gino sat with George Clarke while the wounded men ate their breakfast, eggs, poached with plenty of butter on top, freshly baked white bread, followed by toast with plenty of top-class strawberry jam. 'Christ, George,' he said enviously as he sipped the tea the nurse had brought him together with George's breakfast, 'they certainly do you proud in here, old friend.'

'Fattening us up for the kill again, I should suppose,' George said, egg yolk running down his chin.

'Well, you're looking a lot better since yesterday, even. But I don't know about the kill now, after the knocking-shop business.' He had told his friend about the events of the night as soon as he had been allowed to enter his ward. 'If the Eyeties know we're coming...' He shrugged and said no more.

George looked at him hard, 'Don't be

daft, Gino. Of course the Eyeties don't know we're coming. It'll be a piece of cake. Leave it all to old 'ABC'. He'll work it out, mark my words...'

SIX

There was absolute silence in the Admiral's cabin, as he and his senior officers listened to Lieutenant-Commander Davidson's report. Outside in the harbour, all was noise and activity in the fleet. Ratings in overalls were working hard everywhere. Though most of the fleet didn't know what exactly was going on, the 'buzz' had it that an op. – a big one – was in the offing. The knowledge put new heart into the weary sailors. They laboured with renewed energy and enthusiasm, loading stores, checking everything that might be needed on a fighting op., from ammunition to watertight doors, testing guns, the hundred and one things that had to be done before the fleet sailed out to fight the Italians.

Inside the hushed Admiral's cabin, Davidson started to sum up, 'I am afraid to say, sir, that I cannot give you a one hundred percent certain answer to this question one way or another,' he said carefully, as the staff listened, faces set, hard and worried. 'Do the Italians know we are coming or not? All the women could tell us was that the pimp had been an officer in the Italian Navy. He had provided the house from his own funds and he never took any of their earnings. These two facts could be significant. Where did he get his funds from?' Davidson answered his own question. 'Probably from the Italian Secret Service. Another point the women made was that he liked them to consort with naval men, preferably officers.' Again Davidson shrugged and said, 'Espionage once more?'

'May I ask a question, Commander?' old 'ABC' said quietly.

'Yes, sir. Of course, sir.'

'How long has this establishment existed, in other words, when did the pimp set up the place?'

'At the turn of the year, sir.'

'So before Italy entered the war, Commander.'

'Yes, sir.'

Old 'ABC' nodded and said, 'Carry on, Commander.'

'Well, this is what I can say finally. It is obvious that the place was used to spy on the fleet. Was it used to find out general information, what ships were in harbour, when they sailed and that sort of stuff? Or was it the pimp's brief to find out about the operation on Trafalgar Day?' He stopped speaking and a sombre pensive mood fell on the group of white-uniformed officers, frozen as if in some waxworks tableau.

Now it was absolutely still in the big, white-painted cabin, the floor dappled by the reflection of the sun's rays on the water outside. The only sound was the heavy tick-tock of the wall clock, ticking away the moments of their lives with heavy metallic inexorability.

Finally the Admiral spoke. 'Gentlemen, I am prepared to take the risk. The operation will go ahead.'

There were sighs of relief from the assembled staff. Davidson coughed and said, 'With your permission, Admiral, Intelligence officers are always regarded as being 'nervous Nellies' and inclined to be on the pessimistic side. It comes with the job. But I think, sir, you're right.'

Old 'ABC' gave him a wintry smile and said, 'Well spoken, Commander. Now

Lyster,' he turned to Rear-Admiral Lyster, the new commander of the *Illustrious*. The year before he had commanded the carrier *Glorious* when Sir Dudley Pound had first dreamed up the plan to destroy the Italian Fleet at Taranto. He knew more about the operation than anyone else in the cabin. 'Will you elucidate?'

'Yes, sir.' Big, bluff and unflappable, Lyster strode over to the big map of the Mediterranean on the bulkhead. 'As you gentlemen know, the Royal Navy in the Med. is divided into two groups due to the strategic position of Italy. There is Force H – here – at Gibraltar and the Mediterranean Fleet – here – at Alex. Both of us operate independently, which is not good, this division of forces.'

'Now, it is our intention to join these forces together five days prior to the main operation. They are to be involved in protecting convoys, four in all, going to Malta and here to Alexandria. Naturally the Italians in Sicily and their spies on the southern coast of Spain will note all this activity and report it to Rome. It is our firm hope that the Italian *Comando Supremo* will accept that we're at sea in full force due to this convoy activity. Is that clear?' Rear-

Admiral Lyster barked and shot his listeners a hard look from beneath his bushy, bristling eyebrows as if they were all cadets back at Dartmouth.

'In all we shall have two carriers, six battleships, ten cruisers and thirty destroyers deployed. We think that a force of this size will frighten the Italians. They won't sail from their harbours to tackle that kind of fleet. 'So,' he said with a note of triumph in his voice, 'effectively we'll have them in their ports, especially Taranto, during the course of these convoy operations. Exactly where we want the Italian Fleet, gentlemen.' He squeezed his big right hand as if he were crushing the Italian Fleet to bits.

'Now once we have caught the Italians off guard, we attack in two waves. Each strike will have twelve Swordfish armed with torpedoes. They will be accompanied by six others, armed with flares and bombs – a total force of thirty aircraft then.'

For a few moments he paused to let the information sink in. Then he said, 'Now each torpedo will be armed with the new Duplex pistol firing device–'. He saw the looks on some of their faces and added hastily, 'I know that the Duplex performs badly in anything approaching a heavy sea and there is, too, the danger at Taranto, with its shallow water, that the torpedoes will hit mud and not metal.' He sniffed. 'But the water in Taranto harbour will be calm and even if the torpedo does explode in the mud, it will explode directly under the hulls of the Italian ships. I think those two factors justify the risk of using the Duplex pistol, don't you, gentlemen?'

There was a chorus of assent from most of his listeners and Rear-Admiral Lyster gave them a brief wintry smile before continuing. 'We shall launch the two strike waves, with an hour between each strike, near the Greek island of Cephalonia at a point to be known as "X for X-ray", remember that gentlemen. From now onwards the name of the Greek island is not to be mentioned again even amongst yourselves. *"X for X-ray",*' he emphasised the codeword.

'From "X-ray" to Taranto harbour is exactly one hundred and seventy miles. So we launch our aircraft at twenty hundred hours when it will already be dark and we confidently expect them to be over the target at twenty-two hundred hours. The second wave will reach Taranto just before twenty-four hundred...'

Again he paused to let them absorb the information.

'Both waves,' he went on after a moment, 'will fly up the centre of the Gulf of Taranto. They will approach the enemy base from the south-west. Before the torpedo bombers go in, the four planes dropping flares to illuminate the targets will do their job and there'll be some dive bombing of the Italian cruisers as they have the best anti-aircraft protection.

'While all this is going on, the carrier force will steam up and down off "X-ray". At zero one hundred hours, the carriers will sail for another position, code-named "Y for Yorker". Please memorise the code-name now, gentlemen,' the Rear-Admiral advised severely. 'This will be twenty miles from "X-ray". Here they will be ready to land the returning aircraft.' He breathed out hard, and added, 'And that's about it gentlemen, save for the code-name for the whole attack. The C.-in-C. picked it himself and if I may be allowed to say it, I find it very appropriate.' He looked across at old 'ABC'.

The latter smiled back at him encouragingly.

'All right, gentlemen, here it is. The code-name is "Operation Judgement".'

There was a mutter of approval from the senior officers and someone said, 'Just the thing. A judgement on the whole of Musso's damned navy!' 'Agreed … agreed … well said there,' the others commented enthusiastically.

'Well, then,' Lyster boomed with an air of finality, 'I know it's damned early, but I'm dry after all that chat. I suggest, with the C.-in-C.'s permission naturally, that we adjourn to the wardroom and enjoy a stiff pink gin.'

A few minutes later the mess stewards were astonished to see senior officers, faces flushed with excitement, raising their glasses, big ones, filled with pink gin and crying enthusiastically, 'Here's to Operation Judgement!'

That mid-morning toast helped to heighten the 'buzz'. 'The officers are boozing at ten in the morning,' they whispered to each other knowingly, as they went about their tasks, caps at the back of heads, 'Woodbines' tucked behind right ears. 'Now yer can't tell me, matey, that there's nothing on – we're gonna invade mainland Italy,' they said confidently. 'No use pratting about in the Western Desert, we're gonna to go straight for the old wop's throat. It's Rome,' they said. 'They've already told the Pope he's safe. We're just after Musso and the top Blackshirts. Once we've done with them, them Eyeties'll fold up like a wet paperbag. All be over by frigging Christmas…'

In the harbour the bumboats, which sold fruits and other additions to their diet, to the hungry sailors of the fleet soon picked up the various 'buzzes'. As the day passed, they told what they knew to the skinny-legged fishermen with their turbanned heads and naked legs. Coins changed hands. As dusk fell the fishermen sailed out into the Mediterranean as their forefathers had done for generations. By dawn they hoped to be back, laden to the gunwhales with silver, gleaming fish for the markets of the Place de Mahomet Ali. They also hoped for something else: the gleaming silver Maria Theresa dollars which the Italian submariners gave them for any useful information. By dawn the Italians would know as much about 'Operation Judgement' as the lowly matelots of the Mediterranean Fleet, false as this information was.

SEVEN

'So now, people, we are at war with Greece,'
Mussolini shouted from the balcony at the
great crowd gathered below in the piazza.
'Our brave battalions march on Athens at
this very moment.'

There was a great yell of approval from the
crowd, followed by mass hand-clapping, as
if they were watching some favourite foot-
baller who had just scored a goal.

'We march, too, against the British in
Africa,' he roared, heavy, pugnacious jaw
sticking out, hands on his plump hips. 'On
two continents, as in the days of old, the
Italian soldier is marching, fighting, *winning!*'

There was another great outburst of
cheering and clapping, as the *Duce* stared
down proudly at 'my Italians', as he always
called them when he was pleased with them.

'Today, Italians, together with our Ger-
man comrades, led by my great friend, the
Führer, we dominate Europe and Africa.
Nothing can stop us. We are all powerful.
Anyone – anything – which comes in our

way will be crushed. I salute you, my Italians!' He flung himself to attention and gave the cheering throng below the Roman salute. Then, without another word, he turned and marched back into the coolness of his office.

Servants hurried forward. He was offered a glass of *grappa*, which he downed in one gulp, while another servant sprayed him with eau-de-Cologne. He ripped off his sweat-soaked black shirt to reveal that barrel chest of which he was so proud, ignoring totally the prominent men and women who had been listening to his speech inside the huge room

He slipped into a fresh shirt, after the servant had sprayed more eau-de-Cologne into his armpits, thrust the ends into his black breeches and then smoothing his hands along his bald pate, as if he was thrusting back long hair, he strode deeper into the room. 'Well, sire,' he demanded of the dwarf-like King, who was wearing a huge military shako, which bore a large ostrich feather, in the belief that this made him look taller, 'what did you think of the speech?' Even as he asked the question, his eyes were on the others; Count Ciano, his son-in-law, his sour-faced wife who looked the peasant she had once been, and above all at Clara, his mistress. Seeing his eyes looking at her, she thrust out her splendid breasts provocatively. He could see the huge nipples under the thin silk blouse and told himself that within the hour he would be sucking and fondling them.

'As always, *Duce*,' the King declared in his thin, reedy old man's voice, 'an excellent speech. The reaction of the masses, I am sure, told you that. The Romans,' There was a faint touch of irony in the King's voice, 'have always loved you.'

Irony was wasted on Mussolini. He struck a dramatic pose and declared, 'Yes, they love me, ah yes!'

'However, I am concerned about this new war against the Greeks,' the King ventured nervously. He knew he was a mere puppet in the dictator's hands, but still he was the King. 'Are we not over-extending ourselves?'

The *Duce* stared down contemptuously at the little man in the absurd hat, but he said nothing for the moment.

'I mean, *Duce*, we are at war with the British and our supply lines are endangered by their fleet in the Mediterranean. Only the other day, as you know, they bombed our supply ports in Africa – Tobruk, Tripoli and the like.'

The *Duce* had had enough. 'The British lion is old, sire, and losing its teeth rapidly. We have nothing to fear from that quarter, I can assure you.'

'But *Duce*,' the King tried to continue.

Mussolini gave an impatient wave of his well manicured hand. 'I am afraid, sire, I must go. There can never be any rest for me. There are affairs of state to be attended to.' He bowed and left the King standing there open-mouthed.

The crowd of courtiers, officials, politicians opened to let him pass. As he went through he brushed against Clara's massive bosom. It gave him a thrill. He felt the stirring in his loins. God, he told himself, wasn't he virile? He had the sexual strength of a boy of eighteen. Why he'd already enjoyed her two hours before and now he was aroused yet once again.

Behind him Donna Mussolini, her face even sourer, stared at the mistress with burning hatred. Clara retreated from the fury of that gaze. She bowed and followed the *Duce* hurriedly.

Admiral Iachino, the Commander-in-Chief of the Italian Navy was waiting for him in the huge office when he arrived, accompanied by staff officers and aides. Hurriedly they rose to their feet, as the dictator stalked in and took his seat behind the great marble desk. 'Be seated, gentlemen.' He flashed a glance at his wristwatch. 'You have exactly fifteen minutes.'

The Admiral, long-faced and lined, flushed a little, but said only, *'Grazie, Duce.'* He sat down and his staff followed, arranging themselves awkwardly on the ornate gilt chairs.

The *Duce* put the tips of his fingers to his right temple. The gesture said he was ready to think about whatever the Admiral had to say, 'Proceed,' he snapped.

'Duce,' the Admiral, a veteran of the first war, began, 'I am not pleased with the naval situation.' He waited. Mussolini said nothing. He went on. 'Two fleets, ours and the enemy's, are about equal in numbers in the Mediterranean, though we have the more modern ships.'

'Of course we have, Admiral,' Mussolini said proudly. 'We have the finest and most powerful navy in *Mare Nostrum.'*

The Admiral sniffed and told himself the Mediterranean was certainly not 'our sea', as the *Duce* asserted. More likely it was the

British who dominated the inland sea. Aloud he said, 'But the British have one great advantage over us.'

'What?' Mussolini demanded.

'Two aircraft carriers. We have none.'

'You have the *Regia Aeronautica*.' Mussolini meant the Italian Air Force.

'But the Air Force is land-based and there is little co-operation between it and the Navy. So, if our fleet puts to sea, it is very vulnerable to the attacks of carrier-based enemy planes. So the fleet stays in port where it has the protection of the Air Force. It is not a happy situation for us sailors, *Duce*,' the Admiral added.

'You will be given your opportunity to sail and fight – and *beat* – the English soon enough,' Mussolini declared proudly. 'I have plans for you and your Navy, Admiral.'

'But till then we remain in harbour, in particular, in Taranto where most of the battle fleet is at the moment. There, packed like sardines in a tin, battleship next to battleship, we are a highly tempting target for Admiral Cunningham, the commander of the enemy's Mediterranean Fleet.'

'I have seen a picture of him,' Mussolini said. 'He is an old man. He does not look aggressive. Commanders must be lean and aggressive – he isn't. Besides,' he added scornfully, 'the English are on the defensive everywhere. They have no spirit for the attack.'

'These English sailors, *Duce,* are brought up in the spirit of Nelson, *Duce.* They have it bred into them – *attack.*'

Mussolini gave a contemptuous wave of his hand. 'Nelson is long dead. The English milords have grown old and decadent since his time. What if the English did attack Taranto,' he tried a new approach in an apparent attempt to appease the pale-faced old Admiral, 'eh? Think of the defences, Admiral: three lines of defence; thirteen sound listening posts around the harbour; twenty-one batteries of 75mm guns, thirteen ashore and eight on floating platforms; fourteen heavy machine guns and 121 light machine guns.' Mussolini reeled off the figures happily, proud of his ability to display his knowledge in this manner, knowing that he knew the figures better than any of the naval officers present at that moment. 'In addition you have the firepower of the fleet.' He paused for breath.

Next moment he continued once more, while the Admiral and his staff listened stony-faced. 'Then there is Taranto's passive defence: four thousand three hundred metres of steel anti-torpedo netting around the warships in the inner harbour; twenty-seven barrage balloons already in position, with another sixty-three to come.' He shrugged. 'Let the English come if they wish, but I tell you this, Admiral, they will regret it bitterly.'

Admiral Iachino remained unconvinced. 'I agree, *Duce*, the defences at Taranto are very strong, but one vital thing is lacking: aircraft under my command.'

'Impossible!' Mussolini reacted angrily.

'The Air Force wouldn't agree to taking orders from the Navy. Besides, I can't tie up hundreds of aircraft in the Taranto area just in case the English attack. We need every plane available to help Graziani in Africa.' He looked pointedly at his watch.

The Admiral saw the gesture. He was not impressed. He had been in the Italian Navy since he was eighteen. He loved the service. It was his life. 'Then you will undertake nothing, *Duce?*' he asked sternly while around him his officers froze. One didn't ask such direct questions of the dictator.

Mussolini didn't speak.

'Good.' Admiral Iachino rose to his feet. 'Then, *Duce*, you will take the responsibility when the English come. We will do our best, that is all I can promise.' He reached for his white admiral's cap. 'Gentlemen,' his officers stood up and clicked to attention. The Admiral raised his hand to his cap in salute. 'Then I bid you good day, *Signor* Mussolini.'

Mussolini was too flabbergasted by Iachino's use of *Signor* instead of *Duce,* the leader, that they were almost out of the huge office before he had time to react. 'Damn you, Iachino!' he cried angrily. He seized the inkpot, complete with gold pen, which rested in front of him on the great desk. With all his strength he flung it against the wall. It shattered there with a loud crack. The Admiral and his staff didn't turn round.

In a bad mood, he crossed to Clara's apartments. She was waiting for him as usual. Her plump nubile body was naked underneath the silken wrap. He could see her contours quite clearly. 'Caro,' she whispered huskily. She reached up to kiss him. But he was in no mood for romance and kissing. Brutally he shoved her back on the big bed, with its ornate gold fittings, and tugged at his belt.

In sixty seconds he was naked save for his black shirt. He fell on top of her, ripping open her gown. Her breasts fell out and he squeezed them roughly. She gasped with pain. He didn't notice. With his one hand he thrust open her legs. With his other he guided his penis inside her and poked it into her with all his strength. 'Come, whore,' he commanded, 'fuck!'

But later when he was dressed, rested, having worked off his fury at the Admiral's behaviour on her, he sat at his desk in a kind of daydream. What if the English did attack at Taranto and succeeded in destroying the fleet? What would happen to Italy – to him – then? Suddenly Mussolini, the 'man without fear', as he always proclaimed himself proudly, felt a cold chill of apprehension trickle down his spine…

EIGHT

As Trafalgar Day approached, the men of the Mediterranean Fleet worked all out. Everyone knew, even the youngest ordinary seaman, that something big was on its way. Nightly the Swordfish practised low-level night flying, zooming off into the warm September sky to practise dummy attacks.

As Rear-Admiral Lyster said over and over again, sometimes hammering the table in the briefing room to emphasise his point, 'There's got to be no mistakes. We'll get one bite of the cherry – no more. Hit the target first time!'

While the crews trained, intelligence officers studying the aerial photographs of Taranto, which were being developed daily, now that the new fast American Marylanders were zooming in over the port from their base in Malta with impunity, grew steadily more worried. It almost seemed that the Italians had been alerted on what was to come. More and more anti-aircraft guns were being placed in position and the number of barrage balloons against dive-bombing and torpedo attacks from the air was increasing almost daily. One thing, however, was clear which gave them some encouragement: the Italians had not yet completed laying their anti-torpedo netting around their capital ships and that which had been laid did not reach the bottom of the harbour. Either it was not long enough or the ships' captains had decided it was too much of a task to raise it in case they had to go to sea and had decided to lower it just enough to cover their hulls.

All the same things began to go wrong with 'Operation Judgement'. The *Eagle* which had been repeatedly bombed since the Italians had entered the war had to be taken out of service for urgent repairs and returned to Alexandria. 'ABC Old' Cunningham was furious. But he knew there was nothing he could do about it. The *Eagle* would not be able to keep up with the *Illustrious*, which would sail at thirty knots, once the operation had been completed and the Italian Air Force started to come looking for her. The *Eagle* would simply be a liability and he couldn't afford half his carrier force if she were sunk by the Italians. He ordered that the *Illustrious* should take as many of the *Eagle's* planes as she had room for.

The days passed rapidly. As September gave way to October, strange and alarming reports started to flood into Naval Intelligence HQ. More than one skipper reported he had sighted some sort of strange small craft skimming just feet above the waves. One skipper maintained that one of these mysterious craft had attempted to attack him. '*How?*' he had been asked. 'Well, it was in a funny sort of manner,' the skipper had answered, as if he were finding it difficult to put his thoughts into words.

'Go on,' the men at Naval Intelligence had urged, 'spit it out!'

'Well, the thing came hurtling across the sea – I'd say more in the water than out of it. Like a bat out of hell. Then suddenly it went up in a sheet of flame and disappeared.'

'What did you do then?'

'I hove to and had a look-see and searched for whoever was in the craft.'

'And did you find them?' the men from Naval Intelligence asked.

'No, nothing at all,' the skipper said, ''cept this.' And he produced what looked like a gasmask with a head piece...

Five days later the sirens shrilled urgently at the dockside in Alexandria as a lookout spotted something skimming across the harbour, heading straight for old 'ABC's' flagship, HMS *Warspite*.

Almost immediately the battleship's pom-poms opened up, sending a stream of furious tracer heading straight for the strange craft, while the turret gunners frantically tried to bring their guns to bear on an object more below the surface of the water than on top of it.

One thousand yards ... five hundred ... the strange craft seemed to bear a charmed life, as all around it the sea boiled and erupted with bullets and shells. On the bridge of the *Warspite,* old 'ABC,' cool and unflustered, as always suddenly saw through his glasses two figurers, clad in black, spring over the side of the craft, leaving it to surge on on its own.

Crump! At last a shell hit the strange vessel. It exploded with a tremendous roar in a scarlet flash of high explosive which caused shock waves to run right across the sound. Instinctively old 'ABC' opened his mouth to prevent his eardrums from being burst, and as the shock wave hit his face like a blow from a damp flabby fist, said, 'Two figures baled out of the thing. Apprehend them.'

One hour later a flustered Commander Davidson was reporting directly to the C.-in-C., 'It's a new weapon, sir, totally new.'

'What is it then, Commander?'

'A manned torpedo, so the Eyetie prisoners say.'

'A what?'

Davidson repeated the information.

'But a weapon like that is suicidal,' old 'ABC' objected.

'Virtually, sir,' Davidson agreed. 'In this case the two-man crew were to direct the manned torpedo at your flagship and when they were sure they were on course to dive over the side at the very last moment.'

Old 'ABC' whistled softly, as if in admiration. 'They say the Italians are not particularly brave, but I must say it takes some guts to do a thing like that. Besides how did they know they wouldn't be shot out of hand when apprehended?'

'Exactly, sir. They hadn't a chance in hell of getting back to the sub which brought them to Alex. Yes, I agree, sir, if they *had* succeeded in hitting the *Warspite,* I shouldn't have been surprised, if some junior officer had bumped them off quietly on the jetty.' He looked very glum. 'It's another headache, you know, sir,' he said, voice sombre.

'I know, Commander. If the Italians have those things lurking outside Alex in their subs and their crews are as brave as the ones we picked up, we're faced with a monumental headache.' He shrugged. 'But there's no turning back now. We'll send out more anti-sub patrols and see if we can't deal with them that way.' His face hardened. 'Operation Judgement must go on!'

Three days later tragedy struck the fleet. As Trafalgar Day approached, the striking force of thirty Swordfish were in the *Illustrious's* vast cavernous hangar while mechanics and riggers swarmed all over them. They tested engines. They checked air frames and rigging while the air gunners fitted the overload tanks.

One of the air gunners straightened up for a brief rest. As he did so his foot slipped on the greasy floor of the Swordfish's cockpit. He yelled in alarm. He clutched in vain for a hold. Next minute he fell heavily. As he did so the screwdriver he was holding, touched a pair of exposed terminals in the cockpit. They sparked immediately.

The brightly lit hangar was saturated with petrol fumes from the Swordfishes' engines.

Instantly the spark touched off a flash. The flash an explosion. The whole tail section of the Swordfish disintegrated. In a burst of flame the unfortunate air gunner was blown right across the hangar as the plane went up in flames.

The whole thing had happened in a split second. Now the crowded hangar – the very ship itself – was in dire peril. But the drill for such an emergency had been practised time and time again. Now the fire-fighting crews snapped into action. The spray extinguishers were switched on immediately. Salt

202

water squirted everywhere. The flames hissed and squirmed angrily. Great clouds of steam rose. But the flames were beaten. In a matter of minutes the fire was out.

The damage had been done, however. Grimly the C.-in-C., hurriedly summoned from the flagship, and Rear-Admiral Lyster surveyed the smoking sodden hangar. 'Two Swordfish are write-offs, that's for certain,' Lyster growled, as he looked at the blackened charred planes, most of the fuselages burnt away, tyres flat. 'Several are damaged, and can be repaired, however. But,' he gave a sigh like a sorely troubled man, 'all the others have been soaked with salt water. Not one plane of the whole two squadrons is fit to fly, sir, I am afraid.'

Cunningham was not a man for revealing his emotions. In his long life at sea he had seen many tragedies and much suffering. He had learned to control his thoughts and emotions. But he told himself that this minor accident showed upon what a slender thread of chance hung the whole fate of the British fleet in the Mediterranean; perhaps even the course of the war itself.

Finally he broke his brooding silence. 'What are you going to recommend, Lyster?' he asked, his voice revealing nothing.

Lyster hesitated, as if he couldn't bring himself to say what he knew he had to say. 'Well, sir,' he cleared his throat gruffly, 'it's not for Trafalgar Day, sir. Every plane will have been soaked through and through. So each engine will have to be stripped and taken up to the flight deck where the parts will be washed out with fresh water. All instruments, including the wirelesses, will also have to be taken to pieces, dried, cleaned and reassembled. It's going to be a tall order, sir. With the men working flat out, including the air crew, we're not going to get the "stringbags" ready for Operation Judgement on the day selected. That's it.'

Old 'ABC' didn't hesitate. 'All right, tell Boyd.' He meant the captain of the *Illustrious* to get on with the job. 'We'll pick another date as soon as you report to me that your planes are airworthy.' With that he turned and stalked over to the lift, his face showing no emotion, neither disappointment nor anger.

Minutes later the mechanics and riggers were beginning to strip the sodden engines...

It was the next day that Gino Green and George Clarke reported aboard the *Illustrious,* with Green supporting his friend, who was trying to hide just how bad the limp in his wounded leg was. They found Captain Boyd on the flight deck which looked like an aircraft factory, with parts and spares stacked everywhere and swarming with ratings scuttling back and forth, faces and overalls black with oil and grease.

Boyd's normally immaculate whites were stained too, and he had a smut on his face as if he had been doing some of the work himself. Green and Clarke recognised some of their flying comrades, officers all, working side by side with the ratings. It was clear that everybody was in on this. Captain Boyd looked up as the two of them saluted. 'Glad to see you aboard again,' he said briskly. He eyed Clarke hard. 'How's the nether limb?' he barked.

'Fine, absolutely fine, sir. The surgeon commander at the hospital said I'm fit for flying duties once again.' The surgeon commander had said nothing of the sort. He had said when Clarke had begged him to discharge him, 'You're fit enough everywhere else. The leg is healing well, too. But really it is too early to say whether you can fly with it. Wounds do tend to burst open if too much strain is put on them too early. You understand that?' To which Clarke had answered cheerfully, 'I'll take that chance, sir.'

'All right, then, if you're fit, go and find yourselves some dungarees and report to the chief bosun. He'll find something for you to do, I'm sure.'

Five minutes later, dressed in a pair of ill-fitting dungarees obtained from the purser's office, like two school boys who had just played a successful jape on some forbidding beak, they shook hands, 'Well, Gino,' George Clarke declared, 'we've bloody well done it!'

'That we have, George,' Gino snorted, producing two bottles of ice-cold Rheingold beer from his bag. He pulled out the plugs and handed one bottle to George. He raised his own in toast. 'Here's to a short and happy life, George. Let's hope we make beautiful corpses,' he cried in high good spirits.

They would.

NINE

The wardroom of the *Illustrious* was absolutely packed. Forty-two pilots and gunner-observers sprawled in leather armchairs, squatted on the edges of tables or lounged against bulkheads. Then there were the senior officers who filled the aisle or were seated at the briefing table. The place was loud with excited talk and blue with smoke, as younger officers puffed furiously at cigarette after cigarette while the older ones puffed away at their pipes.

The combined fleet had been at sea for three days now, steaming between Alexandria, Gibraltar and Malta, conveying troops and equipment between those places and so, old 'ABC' hoped, thoroughly confusing the Italians who had been following their various departures and arrivals with their reconnaissance planes. Now this night the great attack would commence and there was nervous tension in the very air, for even the most sanguine of the young officers knew what was at stake.

The pilots, young for the most part, were of all sorts. There was a Royal Marine captain among them. The Royal Marines aboard the carrier had prepared a special 'bomb' for him. It came in the form of a well-worn marching boot wrapped in a brown paper parcel and addressed to 'Musso'. It depicted a naked Mussolini receiving a hefty kick up the backside by a man dressed in peacetime Marine uniform. 'Just to remind the Eyeties that the Marines are in on this show, sir,' the corporal who had presented the captain with the 'bomb' had maintained.

There was 'Gertie', as he was nicknamed, a tall languid youth who affected large flowery silk handkerchieves and squirted liberal quantities of scent on his flying overalls before he took off and was suspected of being 'slightly pansy'. He'd already won the DSC, and bar.

There was a neutral, too – a lanky, gangling American commander in the neat blue uniform of the US Navy who had come to the *Illustrious* on an exchange visit to see how the 'Limeys' did it on their 'flat tops'. The US Congress would have had a fit if they knew that he was now taking part in a British operation.

And there was that half-Italian Gino Green, who was in high good spirits. 'Gawd Almighty, George,' he chortled as he sat on the edge of the chair which he had secured by dint of much shoving in the first scrimmage for seats so that Clarke could rest his wounded leg, 'it seems like ages since we first started on this Taranto caper. Now we're off at last, eh.' He looked down fondly at his old shipmate. 'Nothing's going to stop us this time.'

'No,' George replied, liking the enthusiasm he could see glowing on the little man's face. 'Knock 'em for six, that's for sure.'

'Attaboy!' Gino punched his friend affectionately on the right shoulder.

'*Gentlemen,*' Rear-Admiral Lyster stepped up on a chair so that everyone could see him. 'You know what day this is?'

'It's Monday,' some supposed wit at the back of the wardroom called out to the cheers and boos of the others.

'I know.' Rear-Admiral Lyster took the alleged witticism in his stride. 'But it is also November 11th, 1940, the twenty-second anniversary of the German surrender at the end of the Great War. Not as good as Trafalgar Day–'

– 'I say,' the alleged wit yelled, closing one

eye and putting one arm behind his back in a way which he thought made him look like Nelson, 'I say, I see no signal,' he chortled.

'Put a sock in it, Jumbo,' others cried. 'Let the old man have his say.'

Patiently the Admiral waited for the uproar to die away. He knew these young airmen were living off their nerves. Most of them had been flying and fighting for months now ever since Italy had entered the war. Now they were going into action again. He knew that they were tense and in the English fashion they attempted to defuse a tense situation by somewhat schoolboyish humour.

'–But sufficiently symbolic to suit our purpose, which is as you all know to destroy the Italian Fleet this night,' the Admiral continued.

He paused for a moment. 'Well, you know the main details of this op. I'll just fill you in with the latest information we have from Intelligence.' He looked down at the scrap of paper he held in his big hand. 'There are an estimated 240 anti-aircraft guns now ringing the Italian battleships, which as you already know are protected by the anti-torpedo nets. Fortunately, as we know for certain now, these nets only go down to their maximum draught so that torpedoes can run beneath them. One disturbing new factor is that the Italians have sent up more barrage balloons since we sailed. It could be that some of these might be linked by wires and cables. Air reconnaissance couldn't be sure.'

'Eyetie bastards,' Gino Green swore, and there was a murmur of approval, as someone else said, 'Not quite cricket, chaps.'

The Rear-Admiral allowed himself a wintry smile at the 'not quite cricket, chaps'. Then he said, 'One thing that air reconnaissance did find out is this. There are five Italian battleships in Taranto Harbour, five out of a total of six in the Italian battle fleet. If we knock them out, we'll cripple the Italian Fleet—'

The rest of his words were drowned by cheers and airmen shouting 'bloody good show!' … and 'Musso's got all his eggs in one basket, this time.'

'Now then,' the Rear-Admiral went on resolutely. 'About the return journey.'

But some anonymous philosopher standing at the back cried, 'Don't let's bother about that!'

It was the last straw. The Rear-Admiral gave up as the meeting collapsed in laughter. He knew when he was beaten. He had done the planning and talking. It was up to these brave, if irreverent, young men to do the fighting now. 'Good luck, chaps,' he said and left the wardroom and them to their own devices.

Now the aircrews of the two attack squadrons split into little syndicates to work out the individual methods of attack. The leader of the group to which Clarke and Green were attached advocated an attack from the south-west in line astern. He said, 'That'll give us a straight run in and a nicely spread target. The enemy battleships seem to be lying in overlapping berths from this angle. So even if one of our tin fish veers slightly off course, it's almost certain to hit something worthwhile in an anchorage crowded like Taranto Harbour very definitely is.'

There were some objections to the leader's choice of tactics. Someone said, 'A glide-in like that would bring us pretty close to that concentration of ack-ack guns on both sides of the canal which connects the outer and inner harbours.'

The group leader shrugged. 'It's a chance we've got to take, Frank. Anyway everyone knows that the Eyeties can't shoot for toffee apples.'

'Famous last words,' someone else said.

'There's also those barrage balloons tethered to the barges to the west of the capital ships,' Gino objected.

'Same answer,' the group leader said.

Clarke said nothing. But flying at night, he felt that there was more to be feared from the barrage balloons than the Italian gunners. He decided there and then to take the old 'stringbag' right to the deck when they reached the target. That way he'd avoid the damned gasbags and their cables.

All the same, Clarke thought, as the discussion droned on, he knew the ship's company thought none of the Swordfish would return. They saw that the airmen were thoroughly skilled and capable of carrying out the mission given to them, but would they get back, once the Italian Air Force had been alerted? The Italian fighters were at least a hundred miles per hour faster than the old biplanes. They'd soon catch up with the departing Swordfish on the long flight back to the carrier.

But the thought didn't worry him. This was what he had been trained for, for nearly all his life. If he had to die for the King-Emperor, then he would do so just as his father had done in 1916. He felt sorry for

213

his mother. But she'd survive as 'the oldest landgirl in North Yorkshire', as she called herself in her letters to him. She had that kind of middle class spirit of naval officers' wives and widows, which made them carry on despite all the pain, misery and loneliness.

Finally the impromptu meetings broke up. Soon they would be going down to the hangar for the final preparations. Coffee and sandwiches were brought in, though no one except Gino, who was always hungry – 'if you've missed as many meals as I did as a bare-arsed kid, you never refuse a meal' – ate much.

Gertie, who affected a cigarette holder in the style of his hero, Noel Coward, went over to the battered wardroom piano. After a few minutes idle tinkling, he said in his usual languid fashion, 'I say, chaps, what about this – *Bless 'em all, the long and the short and the tall. You'll get no promotion this side of the ocean, so cheer up my lads bless 'em all...*'

The lusty chorus led them into other old favourites, but none of them the usual wardroom obscene ones for some reason they couldn't quite fathom – *There was jam, jam mixed up with the ham in the quartermaster's stores. My eyes are dim, I cannot see. I haven't brought my specs with me ... followed by I've got sixpence, jolly, jolly sixpence. I've got sixpence to last me all my life. I've got twopence to spend, twopence to lend and twopence to send home to my wife...*

But as the brass clock on the wall indicated that it was already time to go to the hangars, Gertie struck up that sad little college song that all would remember in years to come, those who survived, and the memory of it would always bring tears to the eyes of even the most hardened of them – *We're poor little lambs who have lost our way, baa, baa baa...*

On the way down to the flight deck, Gino and George stood to one side to let the Rear-Admiral pass. 'Ah it's you Clarke and – er – Green,' he said in that hearty manner of his. Lyster paused, 'Good luck to the two of you.' Then with a twinkle he boomed, 'I want you to kick them in the pants for me because the Eyetie admiral in charge at Taranto had the temerity to kiss me on both cheeks before the war. And I didn't like it one bit.'

'Ay, ay, sir,' the two airmen grinned as he moved off, 'We'll do our best.'

TEN

As the sun slipped towards the west on the early evening of that fateful Wednesday, the people of Taranto went about their affairs as normal. Italy had been at war for nearly six months now, but the fighting had affected the Italian mainland little. Dockers streamed out of the harbour and headed for the nearest *osteria* for a *grappa* before going home for supper. The workmen from the booming war factories were doing the same, mingling with those who were coming on for the night shift, shouting at each other, ringing their cycle bells. Off-duty sailors headed for the brothels, where the blowsy whores hung half-dressed from the balconies, smoking moodily, waiting for customers. The first strollers of the evening *corsa* came out and for want of anything better to do, stared at the great shapes of the battleships, with the booms out and little boats plying in between them. All was tranquil and normal. It could well have been peacetime.

Darkness fell. The streets started to empty.

A full moon rose. It shrouded everything in its calm silver light. The blackout came into force, in Taranto strict and disciplined; the patrolling policemen saw to that. Those on night duty took up their posts. In their shelters, the bored gunners and soldiers of the searchlight units played cards or smoked and yarned. Sentries patrolled their beats, collars turned up, for it had become chilled, rifles slung carelessly over their shoulders. There had been many boring nights like this, they knew, ever since the *Duce* had thrown in his lot with Hitler. There was no indication that the night of November 11th would be any different from those which had gone.

Admiral Arturo Riccardi, the Port Admiral, was not so sure. On this evening after his meal he prayed, for he was deeply religious and needed guidance. He liked and admired the English. Indeed he always kept a copy of Southey's *Life of Nelson* on his bedside table and read it frequently. He thought of the English as a nation of seafarers, who, unlike the Italians, were highly unorthodox in their methods. For days now he had been plagued by the thought that they might spring a surprise attack on Taranto, but in Rome the *Comando Supremo*, the High

Command, had poo-poohed his fears. The English had too much on their plate for such attacks, they stated. He had pointed out the mass of English warships currently in the Mediterranean. They had answered in Rome that already these ships were turning back to their home bases in Gibraltar and Alexandria. The massive English force had been needed, Rome stated, to protect convoys from the air attacks of the Italian Air Force, that was all.

Now as the elderly Admiral rose from his prie-dieu, he heard the first distant urgent wail of an air raid siren. His heart skipped a beat. Was it the great attack? Or was it simply yet another English reconnaissance plane from Malta? They came over Taranto almost nightly now.

Routinely the flak gunners swung their cannons round to the expected area of attack. On the ships the klaxons shrieked. The gun crews ran for their turrets, pulling on their anti-flash gear. In the town those citizens still abroad, ran fearfully for the shelters. Still nothing happened for a few minutes.

Suddenly, startlingly, the heavy brooding silence which had followed the 'alert' was broken by the thick crump of anti-aircraft guns. The message was flashed immediately to the aged Admiral: the Fifth Battery Group at Grottaglia had opened fire. But a few rounds had succeeded in driving off the lone intruder. The Admiral breathed a sigh of heartfelt relief. *One plane!*

But the respite was brief.

At nine that night, suspicious aircraft noises were reported from the Santa Maria Di Leuca area, some ninety kilometres from the great port. The Admiral listened to the report and concluded that it was just a single aircraft. All the same, he ordered the local gunners to open fire if they could cone the intruder with their searchlights. They didn't and all remained silent. Still Admiral Riccardi didn't relax his vigilance. He ordered that the alert be continued...

In the hangars the riggers and mechanics worked feverishly. They, too, knew now what the target was. Tired as they were, they worked flat out. Petrol tanks were filled to capacity. The overhead tanks were attached, with an extra sixty gallons. Torpedoes were trundled forward on their trolleys. Their noses had been coated with a thin film of oil as a preservative. Now ratings had fingered in their own messages to the Italians in the oil. *Best wishes from Winnie to Musso!... Just dropping in. Illustrious... The gang's all here* and so on. They were attached and released to the pan below just to check if the mechanism was working perfectly. It was.

Bombs and flares were attached to some of the 'stringbags', as the Marine party appeared, bringing up the brown parcel containing the battered boot. It was led by a drill sergeant and the men slow marched to the waiting aircraft. Gino shook his head in wonder. 'Christ, George, you can say this for the Marines. They do things in sodding style!'

Now, the *Illustrious*, plus her escorts, the cruisers *Gloucester*, *Berwick*, *Glasgow* and *York*, and four destroyers were detached from the main force and started to run for the Greek island of Cephalonia at top speed before the Italians tumbled to what was going on. One by one now the Swordfish, their wings folded, began to go up the lift onto the flight deck. Time was running out now.

Lyster and Boyd up on the bridge were worried. The conditions for flying were perfect. A full moon hung over the water, bathing everything in silver light. It seemed almost as if one could see for miles. But there was one catch: there was no wind. The planes were as heavily loaded as they could be and they needed a wind for take-off. The two officers decided they'd bring the carrier's speed up to thirty-five knots to create an artificial wind over the flight deck. The chief engineer would rage. But there was no other way. Knot by knot, the engines quivering and straining under the pressure, the speed of the *Illustrious* was raised.

On the flight deck the pilots and their observers walked up and down, bracing themselves against the sudden wind, taking their last opportunity to breathe in the salt-laden air. What they talked about, none of them ever remembered: their minds were concentrated totally on what was to come and each was cocooned in his own thoughts and apprehensions.

On the tower the lights were on. The batmen made their appearance. Chock-men followed. The wings of the planes were brought down and secured by the mechanics. It wouldn't be long now.

'Come on,' George Clarke said, 'Let's get back to the old kite.' They passed Gertie, who was singing to himself the popular hit of that year. *'We're off to see the wizard – the wonderful wizard of Oz.'*

Gino Green grinned despite his tenseness. 'That geezer's got nerves of steel,' he shouted above the wind. 'Whatever we think he is, old Gertie, he's got frigging guts.'

And so have you, George Clarke thought, but he didn't tell Gino that. He would have been embarrassed.

They went on their way.

Now the 20,000 ton floating airfield was rushing through the night at top speed. The minutes ticked by. Eight bells sounded faintly over the loud-speaker system. Watches changed. It wouldn't be long now. The first wave of 'stringbags' was in position, ready to go.

At ten minutes past eight the warning Klaxons sounded. The waiting air crew took one last grateful draw at their cigarettes and doused them. They adjusted their Mae Wests. Starters whirred as the fitters, seated in the cockpits of the Swordfish started the engines up.

First to board were the pilots. As each one squeezed himself into the tight cockpit, the fitter standing on the opposite wing helped him to fasten his parachute harness straps and Sutton harness.

The observers followed, each equipped with a canvas bag, containing navigational instruments, binoculars and the like. Again the fitters helped them with their straps and when finished did the same as they had done with the pilots. They slapped each officer on the shoulder, crying, 'Good luck, sir.' Then they dropped to the deck, their part in the operation finished.

For a fleeting moment as they sat in their cramped, dimly lit little world the airmen felt a sense of overwhelming loneliness, a sudden chill isolation from their fellows. Then after a few seconds they started to busy themselves with the routine of pre-flight checks. The feeling fled.

The pilots gunned their engines. They checked magnetos and oil pressures. With practised eyes, they flashed a glance at the complicated array of dials and gauges. Behind them the observers unpacked their instruments and donned the earphones of the wireless sets. The Gosport tubes – the 'stringbags' primitive form of intercom – were plugged in. The pilots called up the men seated a few inches behind them. 'You all right, old boy?' they asked. 'Right as rain, skipper,' would come back the answer. What else could anyone say *now*?

The fitters and the riggers now dropped to the deck, wind beating at their bodies, holding on to the chocks for their very lives. At a signal they would whip the chocks away and the planes would be free to move.

Now the carrier turned into the wind. On the flight deck, the roar of the planes' engines had settled down to a steady purr. With the change in the wind direction, their wings started to rock gently. Hurriedly the watchers gripped their caps. On the bridge Captain Boyd began a running commentary on what was going on for the benefit of the men below at their duty stations. 'Flare lights going on now,' he said. 'Won't be long now... Green light... Signal for chocks away... Signal ... Rev engines... All seem in fine pitch... Won't be long now, I repeat...'

Hunched in his cockpit Clarke waited tensely, eyes fixed ready for the signal. Behind him Gino Green muttered 'Hail Mary... Thy grace ... save us...'

A green flare arched into the night sky to explode in a burst of eerie, glowing un-natural light. The lead plane's Bristol Pegasus engine thundered into full power. Slowly it started to roll forward. Operation Judgement was beginning.

The stage was set. The actors were in place. The drama could commence...

PART THREE

Strike At Taranto

ONE

'Range ready to take off,' the deck officer bellowed through his megaphone.

Suddenly the fairy lights illuminating the flight deck flashed on.

Clarke tensed at the controls. The Swordfish was quivering like a thoroughbred horse impatient to start a race. On the deck, the riggers, lying full length, held on to the chocks grimly. From Clarke's viewpoint the flight deck looked like the backbone of an outsized fish, but he knew this was no fish swimming effortlessly through the water. This was a cunning mechanical device with its many dangers. A second too late and the Swordfish could plunge over the side to its doom, for the carrier wouldn't stop to pick up survivors at this stage of the operation. A sudden change in the wind could also spell disaster. Behind him Gino Green prayed even more fervently.

An abrupt circular sweep of the controller's green torch. It was time to go. Clarke forgot his fear. Instead he concentrated on the job of getting airborne. The Pegasus engine thundered at full power. On the deck the riggers pulled away the chocks swiftly. The Swordfish, released, started to roll down, gathering speed by the instant. Behind Clarke, Gino Green ceased praying. There was nothing he – or God – could do now.

They swept over the side. The Swordfish lurched alarmingly. For one horrifying moment, Clarke thought he had lost her. Then, joyfully, she started to rise and behind the pilot, Gino reached for the Gosport tube and said huskily. 'I thought I was going to shit a brick, George.' His accent was pure cockney at that moment.

George Clarke laughed and replied, 'You weren't the only one, I can tell you... Hello, there's the signal!'

About five hundred feet above them, a signal flare was floating down, fired by the squadron leader.

'The range will close up now,' Clarke said, watching the needle of his altimeter rise. Above him the leader had switched on his navigation lights for better sighting and was circling slowly as the other planes raced to join him. Below the carrier's fairy lights went out abruptly, indicating that the first group had taken off. They were on their own now.

It was now thirteen minutes from take-off. They were one hundred and seventy miles from Taranto. Now, flying at a speed of seventy-five knots, the flight rose, heading steadily north-west. For the pilots it was no easy task to keep formation. There was a moon, but its light was not sufficient to help the pilots maintain their stations.

In the rear cockpit, Gino did his best to help his shipmate. He peered through the gloom, trying to make out the dark shapes of the other Swordfish, while Clarke at the controls strained almost bodily to drag the heavily laden torpedo-bomber upwards.

Now the squadron was spread out behind the squadron leader like a school of ill-disciplined fish. They rose and fell. They thrust forward to keep station, then abruptly throttled back to avoid hitting another plane. Sometimes they throttled back so much that they were on the verge of stalling. Other times they rocked violently, seemingly almost out of control, when they were hit by the powerful slipstream of a shipmate's plane. But somehow they kept plodding on.

At four thousand feet they levelled off.

Now they ran into scattered cumulus cloud. All around them, the fleecy vapour shimmered like silver gauze in the moonlight, but it was deadly cold. Within minutes Clarke found his knees were knocking and his teeth were chattering. Not with fear, but with the intense, biting cold which went to the very bone. But there was nothing he could do about it, save to remind himself it was going to get hot enough soon once they were over Taranto and the Italian gunners spotted them. Instead he concentrated on keeping formation and avoiding a mid-air collision, eyes screwed up as he tried to see the faint blue light of the squadron leader's plane.

The cloud started to thicken. Flying became even more difficult. There was no radio link between the antiquated planes. The only way they could communicate with each other was by a morse key radio. But the observers who worked the primitive sets had been forbidden to use them, save for an emergency transmission.

Still Clarke, grim-faced and blue with cold, knew it was vital to keep formation so that the squadron would be over the target at roughly the same time to start their attacks. Anyone who lagged behind at some distance could expect that the Italian anti-aircraft gunners would be waiting for them – with a vengeance.

They started to rise again. The squadron leader wanted to get above the freezing cloud. Obviously he reasoned, Clarke told himself, that he was going to lose some of the formation if they didn't get above the cumulus. At 7,500 feet the Swordfish finally broke out of the cloud and into the clear, ice-cold silver moonlight.

Clarke looked hard around him. So did Gino. Together they started to count the planes and note their armament. 'As far as I can tell,' Gino said through the Gosport tube, 'there are five carrying torpedoes, including us, plus two flare-droppers and – yes – over there, there's a "stringbag" carrying bombs.'

'Yes, that's about my tally too,' Clarke said a little gloomily. 'We must have lost quite a few planes. Five torpedo bombers and a lone bomber. Not much to tackle the whole of the Italian Navy.'

'Never worry, George,' Gino said heartily, in spite of the freezing cold. 'Press on regardless, that's what I always say.'

'Yes,' Clarke agreed a little reluctantly, 'that's what it's going to be – *press on regardless!*' He glanced quickly at the green, glowing dial of his chronometer. Fifteen minutes after nine. There were ninety minutes to go. Then the fun and high jinks would start. He prayed that the other missing torpedo bombers would catch up by then. Grimly he repeated Gino's phrase to himself once more – 'press on regardless'.

The minutes passed leadenly. The cold was terrible. Dewdrops hung at the end of Gino's pinched nose and he huddled in his seat, trying to avoid the cutting wind, without success. He thought of the time it had taken to get this far and told himself that whatever happened, he had taken, or would take, part in an operation that would rank in the future with what Nelson had done at Trafalgar in 1805. The thought cheered him up and made the cold feel less intense. Perhaps he might even get a gong. That would make his old dad proud of him. First an officer in the Royal, and then a gong. 'Cor luve a duck,' he'd say in that throaty costermonger's accent of his, 'we ain't half going up in the frigging world.'

Up in the front cockpit, Clarke's thoughts were little different. It had all taken so long, he thought. What was to come next, however exciting and dangerous, would be a bit of an anti-climax. All the same, if they could pull it off and sink the Italian navy, it would be a tremendous achievement: the final justification of the Fleet Air Arm, the stepchild of the Armed Services ever since it had been formed. Now a handful of obsolete planes would have done something that the entire Royal Navy or the bombers of the Royal Air Force had been unable to do – sink the Eyetie fleet. Just as with Gino the thought cheered him up immensely.

Ten o'clock. Suddenly, startlingly, a blaze of lights, red, green and brilliant white, to their front. Gino flung a hasty glance at his map in the shaded light of his torch. 'Santa Maria di Leuca,' he said swiftly through the Gosport tube.

Up front Clarke nodded his understanding. 'That means we're getting there fast, Gino,' he snapped. 'We're entering the Gulf of Taranto.'

'That we are, boss,' Gino answered. 'Can't be long now before the shit starts to fly.'

'How?'

'The Eyeties are not all dummies, technically I mean,' Gino replied. 'After all Marconi *did* invent radio and he was an Eyetie. You can bet your sweet life they've got radar as we have. They'll soon be tracking us.'

'You think so?' Clarke grunted and

switched on the overload petrol tank, knowing now that it was vitally important not to have to worry about petty matters such as the supply of petrol in the heat of the battle soon to come. He would need every last bit of concentration for the attack and then the escape. 'Get rid of petty details now,' he told himself.

They flew on, over the lighthouse at Santa Maria di Leuca, its light clearly visible. For Clarke that was a good sign. If the Italians knew they were coming, surely they would have ordered the lighthouse keeper to douse his beam?

Behind him Gino Green was not so optimistic. He searched the sky for the first warning sign, his gloved hands already clutching the rear machine gun, waiting tensely for the trouble to begin. For he knew they wouldn't get away with it much longer. They were flying over Italian waters heading for the country's most important naval base, so surely the Italians would be on the alert? It was as if they were about to attack Portsmouth and the defenders of the great Royal Navy port were all tucked up and sound asleep in their little warm bunks. No, it was all too good to be true.

Suddenly – startlingly – he saw it. Twin jets

of scarlet flame about two hundred or so feet away. He seized the Gosport tube. 'George,' he rasped urgently.

'Yes,' Clarke replied, still concentrating on maintaining his station. 'What is it, Gino?'

'An Eyetie.'

'*What?*'

'To port.'

'Are you sure?'

'Def. *Twin* exhaust flames, and the "stringbag" has only *one*.'

'Christ Almighty!' Clarke exclaimed as he spotted the twin flames and knew that Gino was right. An Italian night fighter, twin-engined, had attached itself to the loose formation and was already, he was certain, jockeying for position. In a moment or two he would start the fireworks, knocking off one plane after the other. For the Swordfish were too heavily laden to be able to under-take effective evasive action. The attack force was in trouble already – serious trouble.

'Shall I give him a burst?' Gino asked excitedly.

'For God's sake *no!*' Clarke bellowed urgently through the Gosport tube. 'We're too close to the other "stringbags". You might hit one of our own chaps.' He thought desperately, wondering what to do, knowing that he had only a matter of seconds to make his decision. 'Listen, Gino,' he said a moment later, decision made, 'we're going to drop out of the formation. We'll make-believe that we're a straggler. Tempting meat for a prowling night fighter.'

'You mean, we're going to offer ourselves on the bleeding silver platter sort of thing,' Gino snorted.

'Exactly.'

'That's frigging suicide.'

'Don't panic. We've got a trick up our sleeve,' Clarke reassured the little cockney.

'What, for Chrissake?'

'Your rear machine gun. The Eyetie will think our machine guns are in the wings just as they are in all modern planes. So to go on the offensive, he'll think we have to turn and face him, engine-on. But he'll not know just how obsolete the old stringbag is with a design that dates, complete with second cockpit machine gun, back to the last war. Let him attack us and he's in for a great surprise.' Clarke ended and started to throttle back.

Behind him, Gino Green wasn't convinced. 'Famous frigging last words,' he muttered to himself and cocked the machine gun.

TWO

Grandi, the leader of the Fascist National Council, was in great form. He stood at the head of the huge festive table, seated at which were the grandees of the Fascist Party and their wives and mistresses, decked out in black uniforms and elegant evening dresses from Milan's fashion houses, alternately gesticulating and stroking his beard as he made his report. 'In Africa that Italian Lion, Marshal Rodolfo Graziani, at the head of two hundred thousand brave fascist soldiers is attacking from Sidi Barrani,' he thundered. 'In a matter of days he will fling the perfidious British back to Cairo. What can a force of thirty thousand British, most of them niggers at that, do against Italy's élite?' He paused, head raised high, beard bristling, to wait for the applause.

It came enthusiastically from all the illustrious guests save from Clara, Mussolini's young mistress. She couldn't clap. For at that moment she was busily engaged with her right hand inside the Duce's breeches,

237

stroking the Leader's rigid penis, something which gave him more pleasure than Grandi's speech.

'In East Africa, the Duke d'Aosta is repelling all attacks launched against him by the English and their South African allies,' Grandi continued. 'In a signal to the Comando Supremo this very morning, his Grace states that he will go over to the offensive before the week is out. In short, comrades, gentlemen, ladies, it is only a matter of time before the whole of North Africa is ours – *Italian!*'

As he applauded with the rest, Mussolini gave the busy, red-faced Clara a nudge. She was working his penis too fast. He wanted to enjoy the sensation a little longer. Besides it gave him a great deal of pleasure to be so brazen before the wives and mistresses present. He knew they knew what Clara was doing with her hand beneath the damask tablecloth and it gave him pleasure. For he knew he could have any of the beautiful women present. They would cuckold their husbands and lovers at the drop of a hat if he gave the signal. Women all over Italy fought to be allowed to spread their legs for the national hero, *Il Duce*. In the past he had even had letters from nuns in closed communities offering their bodies to him for the 'sake of the Lord and Mother Italy.' The thought amused him and he grinned. Clara grinned automatically, too, thinking that he was grinning with pleasure.

'Now, comrades, gentlemen and ladies,' Grandi went on with another self-satisfied stroke of his goatee beard. 'At this very moment, aeroplanes of our brave *Regia Aeronautica* are flying with their German comrades from bases in France. And do you know what their target is to be?' He paused and looked around him with a smug look on his thin face. 'I shall tell you.' He paused again for dramatic effect, before clicking his boots together and flinging up his right hand in the Roman salute. *'Tonight we bomb London!'*

There was excited applause and an out-break of chatter round the table. The name 'London' passed from lip to lip and under-neath the table Mussolini felt Clara pause momentarily, just when he was getting very excited. 'More,' he hissed through gritted teeth, trying to smile at his admiring subjects at the same time.

'Yes, at last we are taking the war to the capital of that drunken, plutocratic sot, Winston Churchill. Now he will learn what fear is when our brave aircrew drop their bombs on the "Mother of Parliaments",' he said the words with a look of contempt on his bearded face.

Mussolini, sexually aroused as he was, felt the time had come for him to make some comment. After all, he told himself, *he* was the leader, not that *poseur* Grandi. 'It will show the world – this raid on London, the first by our Royal Air Force and not the last I can assure you – that we Italians are a nation of adventurers, seafarers, explorers and soldiers.' It was a trite phrase which he had used often enough before, but it received rapturous applause, as if he had just uttered it for the first time. Under his breath he added, feeling himself nearly overcome with ecstasy, as Clara's clever fingers brought him almost to a climax, 'And we are a nation of *lovers,* as well.'

But the course of true love was not to run straight on this Monday night. Suddenly the great doors of the banqueting room were flung open. A colonel in the Imperial Guard, dressed in full uniform, complete with plumed helmet, clicked to attention and announced at the top of his voice as if he were on the parade ground and not at a gala dinner. *'Duce...* It is vital you come to the telephone at once!' He stood there rigidly at attention.

Hastily Clara slipped her hand out of the Leader's breeches.

Mussolini felt his erection disappearing fast. Under the cover of the table cloth he adjusted his flies, watched by the women whose faces showed their envy of Clara all too clearly. 'What is it that is so vital, Colonel?' Mussolini called across the vast room a little angrily. Still he told himself he could have Clara with full pleasure at the end of the meal. He'd make her play some of her other delightful naughty tricks to make up for this moment of disappointment.

'It is Admiral Riccardi at Taranto, *Duce*,' the colonel boomed. 'He asked me to bring you to the phone at once. It is vital, he said, *Duce*.'

Abruptly Mussolini felt a cold finger of fear trace its way down the small of his back. To cover his fear he threw down his napkin angrily and snorted, 'Am I never to have peace? Must Italy always demand so much of me? After all I am only a mere mortal.' He rose and there were tut-tuts of approval from the assembled women, while their consorts looked suitably grave.

241

Swiftly the dictator stalked the length of the room to the colonel, who towered above him in his silver helmet and demanded, 'Where is the phone?'

'In the ante-chamber, *Duce*.'

'Good. I shall take it.' Leaving the colonel to close the huge doors as if he were some flunkey, he strode into the next room, where the phone, all gold and polished ivory, lay waiting for him. He picked up the receiver and barked, 'Mussolini.'

'Good evening, *Duce*,' Riccardi said, his voice very shaky, as if he had just received a severe shock.

'Good evening. What is it? Why do you drag me away from my humble supper?'

'I am very sorry, *Duce*,' Riccardi apologised. 'But I felt it my urgent duty to tell you at once.'

'Tell me – *what*?' Mussolini snapped, as if he were angry. In fact he was shocked himself, for he sensed that something bad was happening.

'Fifteen minutes ago, I received a report from Sante Maria di Leuca that enemy aircraft were passing by. As you know we do not have radar down there, *Duce*, but we have excellent listening posts and they picked up several enemy aircraft proceeding into the Gulf of Taranto.'

Mussolini blustered. 'What is *several* air-craft, Admiral?' he cried. 'I mean what are you telling me? Is this a bomber fleet or is it just the usual reconnaissance planes? They have been coming in from Malta for months, ever since we entered the war.'

'Just several,' Riccardi said a little help-lessly. 'More than that, our listening posts could not say. Just more than one.'

Mussolini forced a dry cynical laugh, though deep in his brain, the alarm bells were jingling. 'More than one – the figment of some conscript soldier's sordid imagi-nation. Probably the man had drunk too much wine before coming on duty.' He laughed again scornfully. 'My dear Admiral, please do not allow yourself to be panicked. We new Italians, you know, are brave and bold, motivated by a clear cold logic. Your generation was far too imaginative. They let their nerves run away with them.'

Riccardi bridled. He knew when he was being insulted. Even his fear of Mussolini and his damned Ovra secret police could not stop him now. 'Then how do you explain, *Duce*,' he asked cuttingly, 'that these planes were coming in from south-east?'

'What is that supposed to mean, Admiral?'

Mussolini snapped, puzzled by the sailor's words.

'If they were reconnaissance planes, as you have suggested, *Duce*, they would be coming in from the opposite direction flying as they do from Malta and its fields,' the Admiral answered icily.

Mussolini's mouth fell open stupidly. He realised that the Admiral had a good point. Was this then not another reconnaissance, but a deliberate attack to come on the Italian fleet at Taranto? Swiftly he recovered himself. As always in such awkward situations, he blustered. 'So, if that's what you think, my dear Admiral, what have you done? You've had fifteen minutes to make your decision. Out with it, man, what are your dispositions?'

Riccardi sighed. Italy's political leader, he knew, would one day sooner or later ruin his beloved Italy, because he could never see reason; he was too full of his own importance. 'I am keeping the defences of Taranto here on alert, *Duce*. I have asked the Royal Air Force to alert their bases, on the littoral as well, though they have not responded to that request.'

'They will,' the *Duce* intervened. 'I shall see to it personally after I have eaten my frugal evening meal. Go on.'

'The Royal Air Force has, however, allowed me one aircraft.' Riccardi emphasised the word 'allow' ironically, but the irony was wasted on Mussolini. 'A night fighter,' he continued. 'It is already airborne. Once it spots the intruders it will radio back to my ship. I shall then take the appropriate action.'

'Excellent, excellent,' Mussolini said, the relief in his voice all too obvious to the Admiral on the other end of the line. 'Then that is all we can do at the present moment. I have full confidence in you, Admiral. I personally think it is all a mare's nest. However, *if* it is – and I must emphasise the "if" – anything more serious I am quite sure that you will take the appropriate measures. Now I must bid you good night.'

'Good night, *Duce*,' the Admiral replied dutifully. The line went dead and Riccardi stared at the receiver, knowing that nothing had been resolved at all. The call had been wasted. All he had received had been the usual Mussolini claptrap and bluster. He shook his greying head sadly. 'Poor Italy,' he murmured to himself, 'poor Italy…'

As for Mussolini, he turned and strode back into the banqueting hall, swaggering as usual in his black uniform and highly polished riding boots, well aware that all eyes were directed at him. He sat down as Grandi sprang to his feet, extended his right arm in the Roman salute and cried above the chatter of the other guests, 'Duce, I salute you! Important news? Victory in the African desert? Greece–'

Mussolini waved for him to stop speaking. With a forced smile on his broad face, he said, 'Nothing of importance. Just an ancient admiral letting his nerves run away with him. You know what the older generation is like?' He laughed easily.

All around the fawning crowd of party members and courtiers did the same, echoing the Duce's precious words, 'You know what the older generation is like?'

Next to him, Clara's expert fingers swiftly unbuttoned his breeches again. She felt the flaccid member and made a tut-tutting sound.

Mussolini's smile broadened. 'Never fear, my dear Clara,' he whispered into her beautiful ear, 'Brave Italy will rise again. It always does.'

It did. As always. Afterwards Mussolini completely forgot about alerting the *Regia Aeronautica* bases...

THREE

Dino, Conte di Cavour, wished he had a mirror in which to see himself at this moment. Of course he knew he was unbelievably handsome with his pencil-slim moustache and his sleek, pomaded, jet-black hair. But at this moment of triumph, he wished he could see his face, set and determined and triumphant, animated by the desire to kill and win. For now he was right among the ancient English biplanes, lumbering on at half the speed of his twin-engined Macchi night fighter.

He knew that Riccardi had ordered him, through his squadron commander, just to report what he found in the sky over the Gulf of Taranto. But he was a fighter pilot not a damned messenger boy. His first duty was not to that old fart of an admiral, but the Italian Royal Air Force. This night his comrades were bombing London. Now he'd show Italy that there were laurels, great laurels, to be gained over the Motherland itself. He thrust the throttle forward. The night fighter surged forward to close with the English straggler.

'He's fallen for it,' Clarke snapped through the Gosport tube, as he eyed the dark shape hurrying towards them in his rear-view mirror.

Crouched behind his single machine gun, Gino hissed, 'I see the bastard. Wait till he tries this one on for size.' He closed one eye and squinted down the sight.

The Conte di Cavour came scurrying in. Gino curled his finger, white-knuckled, around the trigger of his single machine gun. 'Come on,' he urged, speaking to himself, 'come on and get it ... hurry up–'

He stopped short abruptly. Another dark shape had suddenly come between him and the Italian night-fighter. It was another 'stringbag.' In the same instant that Gino spotted the intruder, Clarke did so, too, in his rear-view mirror. 'Don't fire!' he yelled through the Gosport tube. 'It's one of ours!'

'I know!' Gino yelled back unhappily, as the Italian pilot pressed his firing button.

Scarlet flame rippled the length of the Italian fighter's wing. Red tracer, like a flight of angry hornets, sped towards the un-suspecting Swordfish.

The slugs ripped the length of the plane's

fuselage. Gino groaned. Flame and oil were spurting from its ruptured radial engine. *'Jump,'* he yelled dramatically, though he knew that the pilot and his observer couldn't hear. 'Jump for it before it's too late–' the words died on his lips.

With brutal suddenness the Swordfish's nose tilted downwards. In a mad fury it fell out of the sky, trailing behind it fiery sparks and flaming oil as it disappeared into the darkness and its doom below.

'Break radio silence,' Clarke yelled urgently, 'alert the others. Enemy fighter. *Quick!'*

Gino took his hands off the machine gun as the twin-engined enemy fighter soared away, obviously preparing for another sortie – and another kill. Hurriedly he seized the morse key, turned the radio switch on and started transmitting the warning, *'Enemy night fighter … enemy night fighter…'* Then he dropped the key, as if it was red-hot and tucked the butt of the machine gun into his shoulder once more, squinting down the barrel as the Italian plane came soaring in once more. 'This time you're mine, you bastard,' he snarled, preparing for the kill.

Five hundred feet away the Conte di Cavour hesitated. He had one kill. He knew he should report the position of the enemy planes to Riccardi, but that might give his position away and he would dearly love to swagger into the mess later, announcing coolly to his flying comrades, 'Just knocked off two – three – English planes. Easy as falling off a log.' Then he would ask for a large scotch and soda and allow himself to bathe in the glow of their envious admiration. Perhaps in due course, the *Duce* would give him a medal. He'd rather like a medal. *'Porco Madonna!,'* he cursed. He'd go in for another kill and radio the presence of enemy planes over the Gulf after that. Shaking a little with excitement and the thrill of the chase, he pressed the throttles furiously. The Macchi fighter surged forward.

If the Count was shaking with excitement, Gino Green was icy-cold with pent-up fury and resentment. He would avenge his dead comrades, shot out of the sky before they had a chance to defend themselves. 'Come on, you Eyetie bastard,' he hissed through gritted teeth, 'come to daddy.' His finger tightened around the trigger.

Five hundred feet … four hundred … three fifty … two hundred feet… The Italian fighter loomed up ever larger in the ring sight. Now it seemed to fill the whole heavens. Gino's jaw hardened. *One hundred and fifty.* He could not miss at that range. He pressed the trigger. Suddenly the cockpit stank of burnt cordite and the hammering of the single machine gun drowned even the sound of the Swordfish's engine. Bits of metal started to fly from the Macchi. The port engine burst into flames. The other started to splutter and cough, as Gino poured bullets into the fuselage.

Caught completely by surprise at the fact the biplane had a rear-firing machine gun, the handsome young aristocrat panicked. Desperately he wrenched at the canopy, as the glass in front of him shattered into a gleaming blinding spider's web of broken shards. 'Save me,' he yelled. 'Oh please God, save me!'

But God was not on the side of the Italians this night. The canopy was jammed. The Count screamed and grabbed for the controls again. But they were dead. Suddenly, the fighter's nose tipped. He was crashing. He evacuated his bowels with fear. Thus, wet and sticky, petrified, screaming like an hysterical child, he fell to his death.

Admiral Riccardi sat hunched and tense in his cabin, wondering what he should do now. The staff colonel of the *Regia Aero-*

nautica had just informed him that they had received no further signals from the young pilot who had been sent up to investigate the sightings made at Santa Maria di Leuca. But one of the coastal listening stations further up the coast *had* heard the sound of firing, faintly but distinctly. The information didn't seem to worry the Air Force colonel; he was more concerned about informing the King of the young pilot's disappearance. 'After all, Admiral,' he had said over the phone, 'he is the great-nephew of the Cavour who helped found modern Italy – and His Majesty *is* his godfather.'

A worried Riccardi had mumbled something appropriate and then said, 'But can't you send up another fighter to check?'

'Definitely not,' the air force man had replied. 'I haven't the authority. Besides it would cost me my head if I called the *Comando Supremo* at this time of night and asked for my chief. He's probably out at dinner and as you must understand I couldn't disturb the chief when he was eating.'

Riccardi had groaned and put down the phone with a bang. 'God damn it,' he had cursed to himself, 'here we are in the middle of a total war and all the top people, from Mussolini downwards, can think only of their bellies.'

Now alone in his cabin, the only sound the steady tread of the sentry outside, Riccardi tried to make up his mind what to do next. He knew that if these mysterious planes were coming to attack his fleet at Taranto, they had several advantages on their side. It was full moon and the fleet was at anchor, packed together tightly like sardines in a tin. The capital ships would be unable to man-oeuvre, for their boilers were without steam. Of course, he could order the fleet to get up steam – perhaps even sail from Taranto. But if he did and the English weren't attacking he would look an absolute fool. The whole of Taranto would ridicule him. No, he couldn't do that. So what was he to do?

The ageing Admiral knew quite well, *if* anything went wrong this night and the fleet were attacked, it would be his head that would roll. Both the *Duce,* who knew noth-ing of naval affairs anyway, and the Air Force would blame him. It had been his responsibility and he would have failed to carry out that task.

He frowned. Then he picked up the telephone once more and called his senior aide. 'Carlo,' he barked, trying to appear confident and sure of himself.

'Admiral?'

'Alert the batteries at Cape San Vito and San Paolo Island to stand by.'

'Stand by, sir?' his aide echoed in bewilderment.

'Yes, you heard, Carlo. Tell the commanders that they are to expect an aerial attack this night.'

'But the men will be at their supper–'

'Damn their suppers,' the Admiral snorted angrily. 'Is that all we Italians do – *eat?* Then telephone each of the battleship captains – even if they are at the trough,' he added cuttingly, 'and get their personal assurance that their anti-torpedo netting is in place. At the same time I want a written record from you of each of their replies. Don't forget that, Carlo, I want it in black and white on paper. I am not taking the blame for other people's carelessness. *Claro?*'

'*Si, Claro.*'

Riccardi put down the phone, telling himself he had done the best he could. He loosened his stiff collar and pulled down his black tie. Now all he could do was to wait. He sighed and told himself it was going to be a long night.

Fifty miles away, the attack formation had bunched together once more, the observers now signalling to one another, knowing that they had been spotted and it was useless to pretend that they were not there. Up in the pilot's cockpit, a worried Clarke kept flashing swift looks to left and right, ready for the first appearance of the enemy fighters. For as he had just said to Gino, after congratulating him on his 'kill', 'Surely the Eyeties will have scrambled their fighters by now. I know the Eyeties are supposed to be slow, but they can't be that ruddy slow.' A sentiment with which Gino Green agreed.

But as the minutes passed in tense expectancy, there was no sign of enemy planes. Instead the moonlit sky above the clouds was empty of any aircraft save their own. In the end the squadron commander ordered, 'Close down all sets. I think we've got away with it, chaps. The Eyeties haven't cocoaed.'

And apparently he was right. They hadn't been 'cocoaed'. The 'stringbags' were flying towards their target without any opposition.

Another ten minutes passed. They started to descend. They went back through the damp, freezing cloud and emerged at some 4,000 feet above the Gulf of Taranto. Clarke gasped. A lone plane was circling just below. Then he saw the dark shape of the torpedo

255

beneath its undercarriage. It was another 'stringbag', one of those which they had lost earlier on. Its pilot had probably flown low, directly for the target, and he had made better time because of it.

They came lower still. Now by straining their eyes they could make out the dark curve of the land. 'Won't be long now, sir,' Gino said cheerfully, 'All aboard for the Skylark!'

'Too true – all aboard for the Skylark,' Clarke echoed, concentrating on the task at hand.

Five thousand feet … four thousand five hundred … four thousand… They were coming down fast now, dragged down by their heavy loads. Still all was silent. The sea glittering in the silver moonlight, was empty. Even the usual little fishing boats with their carbide lamps at the bows were missing. It seemed as if the whole of the Gulf of Taranto was asleep. Clarke, busy with the controls, felt a growing sense of optimism; they were going to pull it off!

Up in the squadron leader's plane, his observer asked, 'Four thousand, shall I detach the flare-dropper?' He meant the plane which was to drop the flares which would light up their targets.

'Yes please.' The reply was quietly polite, as if the squadron leader had been offered a cup of tea in the wardroom of the *Illustrious*.

The observer squirmed around in his tight leather seat and flashed the letter 'G' in morse twice to the flare-dropper.

Clarke caught and read the signal, too. His heart leapt. 'Gino,' he called urgently through the Gosport tube, 'the boss has just signalled "G" for "go". *This is it, hold on to your hat!*'

FOUR

On board the *Illustrious*, everyone from the most junior rating to Admiral Lyster himself waited tensely for news of the great attack. The off-watch riggers and mechanics couldn't sleep in their hammocks. Instead they lounged in the hangar smoking fitfully and chatting, every now and again cocking their heads to one side, as if listening for the sound of returning engines. Above them on the pitching flight decks, the pilots and ob-servers of the second assault wave stood by their aircraft, smoking too and staring into the moonlit night, wondering.

Below in the galley, the chief cook was preparing a special cake for the crews when they returned. It would form the centre-piece of the wardroom table, which was already decorated with a notice, drawn by the chief steward, stating *'Welcome Back!'* The chef's *pièce de résistance* was to be an outsize cake, with, in the middle, a sculpted Swordfish made of pink icing sugar.

Admiral Lyster was not so sanguine. He slumped at the edge of the bridge, wrapped in a cocoon of his own thoughts, listening to the throbbing beat of the carrier's engines, the incessant hum of the ventilation fans and the soft hiss of the water over the great ship's hull.

His thoughts were not pleasant. He had been there as Captain Boyd had given his last briefing to the aircrews just before take-off. Usually Boyd said, when the men were about to fly on some mission or other, 'Don't take any unnecessary risks. Get back safely. That's the most important thing.' This time he had barked, with unaccus-tomed ferocity for him, 'I don't want to see any of you back until you have sunk the Italian fleet in Taranto harbour. That's all.'

Now Lyster wondered just how many of

those brave boys would return. Now as he slumped there, listening to the throbbing of the engines, while Boyd stood at the far end of the bridge, empty pipe clenched between his teeth, as if they were bitter enemies, he told himself that they would be lucky if half the crews returned to the *Illustrious*. With the firepower the Italians possessed, one had to accept there would be at least fifty per cent casualties. Still Lyster told himself that it had to be done whatever the cost. For him it was not just an attack on an enemy he despised. The success of this operation would be resounding justification of his faith in the Fleet Air Arm; that air power was capable of tackling great capital ships and destroying them. In essence, this operation would prove, if it were successful, that the day of the battleship was over.

While Boyd and Lyster brooded, telling themselves that this night they had sent a lot of brave young men, men of promise, to an early death, those on duty went about their tasks catfooted, as if they felt that any noise might alert the Italians to what was coming their way. On the bridge the duty officers didn't speak and when they gave orders, they did so in a low voice. Once a rating, coming up the slippery steel ladder, missed a rung. Nerves, tense and highly strung, jarred. A dozen pairs of accusing eyes stared at the red-faced sailor when he entered the bridge.

Now Lyster started to look at his watch every few seconds. He knew he ought not to. It was a sure sign of nerves. But he couldn't help himself. Soon the attackers had to break radio silence with those two words which would tell him that the operation had finished, but not how it had gone – *'Attack Completed'* – God in Heaven, when would that damned signal come through?

The flare-dropper swung round in a lazy circle. He had dropped his first flare at three thousand feet one minute before. The time the pilot noted was exactly two minutes past eleven o'clock. Now the great incandescent white flare was blazing furiously, illuminating the harbour below. The flare-dropper now started to drop his other eight flares at half mile intervals, knowing as he set about the task that he'd soon get some stick, once the Italians spotted him.

He didn't have to wait long. Suddenly the enemy anti-aircraft batteries on Cape San Vito opened up. What looked like glowing golf-balls, gathering speed by the instant, sped towards the lone Swordfish. Search-lights clicked on. Their icy white beams roamed the night sky, trying to find and cone the intruder. The Swordfish pilot pressed on with his task, eyes narrowed to slits against that blinding light, as more and more guns opened fire so that it appeared he was flying through a wall of exploding steel.

Behind the flare-dropper, the other attack planes waited, each pilot straining to pick his own target, hardly aware of the shells whistling by them now. For like all pilots, they had a totally unjustifiable belief in their own immortality. Besides most of them had too much on their hands just flying the heavily laden planes without crashing into shipmates to worry about the flak.

Clarke shot a glance behind him. Gino was ready and eager for action, he could see that in the glowing darkness, which hollowed the little cockney's face out into an unreal death's head. He nodded his app-roval and tried to spot his target among the massed ships. There it was! He remembered it instantly from the recognition book, *Jane's Fighting Ships*. He grabbed the Gosport tube with his free hand. 'To port, Gino,' he yelled above the roar of the flak, which was streaming upwards now in multi-coloured burning fury, 'A *Littorio* class, isn't it?'

'You betcha,' Gino yelled back enthusiastically, 'the latest – all thirty-five thousand tons of her. Are we going for her, George?'

Clarke grinned to himself, 'Now what do you think, Gino?'

'Well what are we gonna do about those frigging barrage balloons? They're every-frigging-where?'

'Well, we'll have to frigging well dodge 'em, won't we?' Clarke cried, echoing Gino's words. 'Here we go!' He thrust home the throttle and set the Swordfish into a steep dive. With a fiery howl they roared lower and lower. The harbour raced up to meet them. There was flak everywhere. A 'flaming onion', all awesome glowing sudden death, sped towards them. At the last moment, Clarke dodged the shell and roared on. The altimeter needle raced round the dial, as that death-defying dive became ever steeper.

He knew he had about a three mile run-in to attack the Italian battleship. To survive that in the face of the intense flak fire, he had to come down almost to the deck. Face grim and set, but at the same time animated by an almost impossible excitement, he came lower and lower. Behind him Gino tensed as the flak whistled by them and Clarke told himself that for him the sensation was probably like careering down a very steep hill as a passenger in a car without brakes being driven by a learner driver. Very unpleasant!

Two Italian destroyers below, lean grey shapes, were firing at him at almost point-blank range. Their gun flashes blinded him momentarily. When he could see again, he saw he was among the barrage balloons. Their dangling wire cables, designed to sever a plane's wings, were hanging on all sides lethally.

Now the flak all along the quayside where, in what seemed another age now they had rented 'Irma's Place' for the day, erupted into bursts of furious savage fire. To port, on Taranto Island, another battery was blasting away at him, as he skimmed the surface of the *Mar Grande*. Desperately he wrenched the stick to the right, as a barrage balloon loomed out of the gloom like a great silver elephant. There was a loud crash. The whole plane shook. 'Christ, George,' Gino exclaimed in awed shock, 'that was some flying. You went just under the fat cow!'

'Yes, and probably lost my undercarriage

to a cable in the process,' George Clarke shouted back through the tube. 'But no matter.'

Now he sped across the surface of the water like a great grey moth. Shell splinters and duds were falling into it all around. Great spurts rose and fell. Massed machine guns on the top of one of the harbour sheds were firing a mass of white tracer at him in a kind of lethal morse. Still the antiquated biplane seemed to bear a charmed life. Time and time again, it missed disaster by mere inches.

To port he saw a 'stringbag', whose he would never know, stagger as if it had just run into an invisible stone wall. Clarke groaned out loud. The Swordfish broke in half in a ball of flame. Next moment it fell out of the sky and dropped into the harbour in two great splashes. Nobody got out. They had suffered their first casualty. Behind him Gino commented laconically. 'Poor sods. Gone for a Burton!'

Clarke didn't reply. He was too busy. Before him lay the inner harbour containing the battleships. Just ahead of him, the squadron leader was going into the attack. He had targeted a *Cavour* class battleship, old but refitted quite recently and some

25,000 tons. Clarke saw how the squadron leader was swinging the heavily laden torpedo plane from side to side, trying to dodge the intense enemy fire. It was a tremendous piece of flying.

Suddenly the squadron leader gave up his weaving and flew a dead-straight course. He was going into the final stage of his bold, daring attack. Now he was easy meat for the enemy gunners. They poured a furious hail of fire at the little plane skimming along the surface of the inner harbour. How anybody could survive the fury and ferocity of that fire, Clarke didn't know. But the senior officer did. At a range of seven hundred feet, he released his torpedo. Clarke could see how the Swordfish rose steeply into the air as it was relieved of the weight of the tin fish.

The deadly weapon struck the water with a great splash. In that same instant the squadron leader wrenched the 'stringbag' round in a complete left-hand turn. But Clarke was no longer watching the 'stringbag'. His whole conscious being was concentrated on the torpedo, as he counted off the running seconds automatically.

Suddenly, startlingly, the *Cavour* reared up out of the water in a blinding burst of angry red flame. Its radio mast tumbled. Electric sparks ran the length of its deck. Dark shapes, sailors, flung themselves over the side in panic right into the steaming, bubbling hissing water.

'*A hit!*' Clarke cried in triumph.

Like the breath of hell, the batteries concentrated their fire on the daring attacker, now hurtling away from the scene of the assault. Scorpion whips of tracer lashed the air all around him. But the Swordfish skidded over the belching muzzles of the anti-aircraft guns. Then – blessedly – he was gone, swallowed up by the darkness, heading back to the *Illustrious* – and safety.

Now it was their turn. Clarke grinned vindictively. The volume of fire was so intense and so confusing that a big Italian cruiser to starboard was pouring its shells right into a group of harmless Italian merchantmen. Already one of them was sinking and another was being ripped by a great searing blowtorch of flame.

'Mussolini,' Gino exclaimed wildly, carried away by the unreasoning atavistic blood lust of battle, 'here goes your number two. Press on regardless, George!'

FIVE

Now after the sinking of the *Littorio* class battleship, the cruisers and destroyers had started firing a cone of shells above the other capital ships as the surest form of protection for them. Clarke made a quick decision. 'Gino,' he yelled through the Gosport tube, 'I'm going to go below that umbrella of fire. Are you game?'

'Course I am,' Gino yelled back almost angrily.

'All right then. Here we go!' Clarke brought the plane down even lower, his prop wash churning the water into a fury a few feet below him.

It was a terrifying experience. Shells were whizzing and exploding just above him showering the ancient plane with red-hot pieces of shrapnel. More than once the fuse-lage was pierced. A wing strut snapped. His aerial was shattered and the wire trailed behind him as he headed straight for the target.

He turned slightly south-east, still flying

under the fiery umbrella. There, before him, lay the finest target he had ever seen. A *Littorio* class battleship, anchored so that she offered a perfect beam shot. Even a one-eyed Chinaman couldn't miss a great target like that.

Now flying a bare ten feet above the surface of the harbour, he headed straight for her. Eight hundred yards ... seven hundred yards ... six hundred and fifty yards. He was close enough. He loosed the torpedo and felt the plane rise a good twenty feet at the release of the great load. 'Give the lad a clay pipe,' he yelled exuberantly, for he knew his tin fish couldn't miss at that range.

A split second after he pressed the tit, Clarke banked steeply to starboard. He was just about to straighten out when he was shocked to see some kind of fishing smack heading towards the Swordfish on a collision course. Instinctively he jerked the stick over. Horrified, he saw the smack's mast rush by the cockpit with only inches to spare. He gasped.

But there were more troubles ahead. This new course brought the battered Swordfish between two of the cruisers anchored to the west of the battleships. They were hammering away into the sky with every gun they possessed. Throttle wide open, he roared over their decks with so little clearance that the blast of their guns almost threw him out of his seat.

Then they were past and with a tremendous roar the *Littorio* class battleship went up as the torpedo exploded right under its hull. The *Littorios* had, as Clarke knew, three supposedly torpedo-proof bulkheads. But they didn't stop the effect of that exploding torpedo. The *Littorio* reeled to one side, her masts tumbling to the debris-littered decks. Minutes later she started to settle at the bottom of the harbour. Mussolini had lost battleship number two.

Now they came in, one by one, braving that maelstrom of fire, each antiquated byplane running that terrible gauntlet of fire as it tried to attack the battleships. Another observer spotted a *Littorio* class. 'That's a *Littorio*', he yelled excitedly through the Gosport tube.

'Right then that's our meat,' the pilot boomed. He drove the plane directly at the great battleship. Now he was zooming in at mast-top height through an incredible crossfire directed at him by the cruisers, shore batteries and the battleships themselves. 'Christ', he cursed, 'they'll be throwing the kitchen sink at us next.' He wrinkled his nose. The very air stank of burnt cordite and burning incendiary bombs.

He pressed the torpedo release tit. Nothing happened!

Now the enormous hulk of the *Littorio* seemed to fill the whole world, as her guns flashed and barked. It seemed nobody could live in that world of driving, red-hot steel and smoke.

Feverishly the pilot re-cocked the release grip. He pressed once more. The 'stringbag' rose high into the air. The tin fish was on its way. He broke off. Suddenly the plane staggered. Behind him the observer yelled. 'We've been hit!'

But they hadn't. Their undercarriage had touched the water and that had staggered with the impact. Now the plane flew on at top speed, racing down that fiery corridor, trying to reach the open sea before it was too late. Behind it another *Littorio* started to sink.

Gertie went in. He was carrying armour-piercing bombs. Below him he spotted a perfect target, a destroyer, clearly outlined and not firing at him. He pressed the bomb release. Six bombs fell like deadly metal eggs from beneath his wings. They just missed the target and then the last four hit the destroyer's deck. Nothing happened. The armour piercing bombs had simply gone straight through the destroyer's thin wooden decks. 'Oh my sainted aunt,' Gertie exclaimed in dismay, 'I do wish I'd joined the ruddy army now!'

He turned away in disgust. Before him lay a mile of fire and flame before he could reach the open gulf. He chortled something about 'the gallant six hundred' and then yelled to himself, *'Charge!'* Now he was going flat out, skimming across the surface of the sea, churning up the water into a white fury with his propeller.

Ahead two barrage balloons, tethered to lighters below, loomed up, vast glistening shapes in the lurid glow of the flames and anti-aircraft fire. 'Whoops', Gertie yelled, and dived even lower. He just managed to scrape beneath them, missing their dangling cables by inches. He grinned. 'Thought you had me that time–', the words died on his lips. The plane rocked violently. Next instant the port wing broke off. It fluttered to the water like a metal leaf. A second later the damaged Swordfish went into a steep dive, heading straight for disaster.

Still the others pressed home their attacks. Now the whole area was carpeted with angry gun flashes and burning shells, shot through with dazzling ribbons of green, red and brilliant white tracer. It was a tremendous waste of ammunition. But the panicked Italian gunners thought that they were being attacked by dive-bombers from all sides so they fired blindly at anything that moved, real or imaginary.

Another 'stringbag' was hit. Still it remained airborne. Before it there were two *Littorio* class battleships and four smaller *Cavour* class ones, formed up in a great square. Beyond lay the jetty, with barrage balloons flying about it in a semi-circle. The pilot of the hit plane made a lightning decision. If he took his 'stringbag' between all four of the smaller warships, he knew he might have a chance to turn, level out and get off a beam shot at one of the *Cavours*. But if he did attempt that he might well be blown out of the sky before he had the chance.

The alternative was to try a risky angled shot at the most southerly of the *Littorio* class ships. He made the snap decision. He would try for an angled shot at the *Littorio* whose quarterdeck he could now see.

Thirty feet above the water the pilot of the damaged plane levelled off, his engine spluttering badly. He ignored the alarming noise.

At five hundred feet, the pilot pushed the tit. The battered plane jerked violently, as the torpedo dropped. The pilot pulled the plane round in a tight turn and started to race for the exit to the harbour. It seemed that every gunner in the Italian fleet took up the challenge, determined to knock the bold intruder out of the sky. Fire poured upwards on all sides. The 'stringbag' was hit again. It rocked violently, but stayed in the sky, its canvas flapping where the 40mm shells had torn a great hole in her fuselage. She was hit again and again. But the old plane seemed indestructible. She continued flying. Then she was through and on her way, heading for the outer darkness of the Gulf of Taranto and safety.

Behind in the burning anchorage lay two battleships sunk and beached, two cruisers sunk, numerous fleet auxiliaries badly damaged, on fire or sunk. And in fifteen minutes the second wave of strike aircraft were due from the *Illustrious* to continue the destruction of the hapless Italian fleet.

Now the surviving aircraft were spread all

over the Gulf of Taranto, each one making its separate way back to the carrier some one hundred and fifty miles away. The crew's sense of elation at the great victory they had scored had vanished now. It had been replaced by a worried sensation of being all alone in the glowing darkness, with every man's hand against them. For all of them knew that the Italian air force must have been scrambled by now. After all the attack had lasted a good thirty minutes, and even the Italians, slow and relaxed as they were supposed to be, would have got their planes airborne in that period of time.

In the rear cockpit, Gino swept the horizon routinely, searching for the first double glow of an exhaust, flames which would indicate a twin-engined enemy night fighter. But the night sky remained empty and slowly Gino started to relax. Perhaps after all the Eyeties didn't yet have radar to locate planes at a great distance and had to rely on visual contact as the Royal Air Force had been forced to do until 1937. He slumped a little lazily in the cockpit, keeping his head low and out of the freezing wind.

Clarke felt exhausted. It was as if an invisible tap had been opened and all energy had been allowed to drain from his body. He knew why. It was the physical effort of that bold bombing run when the adrenalin had been running high. But he forced himself to concentrate on his instruments, the green-glowing dials banked high on the panel. He knew they still had a long and dangerous flight in front of them before being confronted by the equally dangerous task of landing on the dimmed out deck of a carrier travelling at twenty-five knots. No, he told himself, there was no place for relaxation or complacency at the moment. They'd be able to relax once the battered old 'stringbag' was safely below the flight deck of the *Illustrious* in the great echoing hangar.

They flew on.

In Rome it was now midnight. In the operations room of the *Comando Supremo*, telephones jingled incessantly, teleprinters clattered and worried-faced staff officers in their elegant uniforms came and went, bringing ever more alarming news. The head of the Italian Navy sat wooden-faced and silent, a cigarette burning unnoticed in the overflowing ashtray in front of him as the mountain of reports grew and grew.

In this moment of catastrophe he was trying to remain calm and in control. But it was difficult as staff officers, faces set and sombre, reeled off the names of vessels sunk and damaged.

'*Duilo* hit, sir,' said one.

A moment later. '*Cavour* holed and taking water fast.'

'Two torpedo strikes on the *Littorio*.'

When he heard that Italy's latest battle-ship, the pride of the Fleet, had been hit, the Admiral had to grit his teeth to prevent himself from groaning out loud in front of his staff officers.

'A bomb has penetrated the deck of the *Trento*, sir.' Yet another damage report was thrust under his nose.

'The *Libeccio* has been hit—'

The Admiral could not stand it any longer. 'How could it happen?' he moaned out loud. 'Three battleships, a large cruiser, and a fleet destroyer, all damaged, perhaps mortally – all in the space of a few minutes!'

But there was worse to come. A pale-faced staff officer burst into the operations room, crying, 'The English are attacking again. The *Littorio* has been hit for the third time, the *Cavour* is sinking and the *Littorio* and *Duilio* are barely managing to stay afloat. Fires are raging in the seaplane base, the dockyard, the oil storage tanks and in the merchant fleet—' he stopped, gasping for breath, as if he had just run a great race, unable to continue.

The Admiral looked at his staff, his eyes wide and bulging, 'We have lost a great battle. I cannot foresee the consequences. Can we recover from this huge naval defeat?' Then he buried his face in his hands and began to sob...

SIX

At one o'clock precisely on the morning of 12th November 1940, the *Illustrious* and her escorts reached the 'Y for Yorker' position, some twenty miles off Cephalonia. Closely followed by her two destroyers, the carrier raised her speed to twenty-five knots and headed into the wind towards the rendez-vous spot.

Down below the radar operators went on duty, each man crouched before his green-glowing screen, with a tin of fifty Capstan cigarettes at his side, chain-smoking, and searching for that tell-tale spot which would tell him that the planes were coming back.

At twelve minutes past one, the chief radio

operator stiffened like a pointer. He peered keenly at his screen. A blip had appeared on it. Yes, there was another one … and yet another. He stubbed out his cigarette rapidly. He grinned. Turning to the radarman nearest him, he snapped, 'Get on the blower to the bridge and tell 'em, our boys are coming back.'

Up on the bridge Boyd sprang into action, once he received the message. His night glasses were raised and he started to scan the sky to the west. The action seemed to act as a signal. The whole of the bridge and indeed the ship itself came to life suddenly. Air look-outs strained their eyes upwards. Gun crews scrambled to their feet and did the same, willing as many planes as possible to return. In the hangar and engine shop the weary mechanics and riggers roused themselves and hurried up to the flight deck. Now the whole crew of the *Illustrious* was awake and waiting in nervous tension at what the next few minutes might bring.

The fire and crash parties assembled. The 'batman' hurried into his gear. Now they could all hear the sound of plane engines clearly. On the bridge the yeoman of signals cradled his Aldis signal lamp over his left arm, ready to acknowledge the planes' recognition signals as they started to circle overhead.

The first plane flashed its signal. Below the wake of the carrier stood out like a pale ruler against the grey-green colour of the sea. The pilot dropped his flare and circled one last time. Suddenly the carrier's deck turned a brilliant white as the pillar and deck lights were switched on to mark the line of approach.

The watchers tensed. This was it. What would they see? Battered planes and bloody, wounded crews. The 'batman' tensed, his arms extended fully from his shoulders – the OK signal.

The first pilot sighed with relief. He pulled the throttle back and dropped. A moment later his wheels brushed the deck. They bounced once. A jerk. The arrester wire had caught the plane. They were down safely.

Almost immediately the weary pilot and his observer were surrounded by an excited, cheering handling party, who slapped them on the back, offered them lit cigarettes, firing questions at them all the time. *'Did you finish off the Eyeties... Any of our chaps buy it ... where's the rest...?'*

But now the rest of the 'stringbags' were coming in at thirty second intervals and the intelligence officer pushed his way through the excited throng to rescue the airmen, ordering them to report for debriefing at once.

A weary pilot brought his plane in too sharply. In his excitement at being back and safe, he crashed his engine into the tail of a taxi-ing Swordfish in front of him. On the bridge Captain Boyd was about to send a messenger to bring the offending pilot to him when he caught himself in time. He thought, 'Hell, you've done damned well tonight, my lad. I haven't the heart to give you a rocket after all you must have been through.'

By two o'clock that morning, eleven aircraft of the first strike had returned. The number exceeded everyone's wildest dreams. Lyster and Boyd were overjoyed. But who was still missing?

Inside the carrier the debriefing room was a fug of blue smoke, packed with excited aircrew all talking and shouting at once, as the sweating harassed intelligence officer tried to extract the information he needed from the pilots and observers. *Hell of a lot of flak, sir,* they said. *Barrage balloons everywhere ... took off a bit of my wing... Got a good run at the Littorio class... Flew my approach at thirty feet above the drink...*

Piping hot cocoa spiced with rum, was brought in. The aircrews started to settle down. At last the Intelligence officer started to get the information he needed. 'Did anyone see what happened to Williamson?' he asked.

'Last saw him at four thousand feet over San Pietro island.'

The Intelligence officer pursed his lips. 'Doesn't sound so good.'

'Gertie bought it, too,' another pilot ventured. 'Went in low, but fire from the Eyetie cruisers got him. No one baled out. Went straight into the drink. Got the chop.' The words were said with apparent carelessness without any apparent emotion, but all of them knew they could have been in the missing men's position and felt for them. There'd be no gongs or commendations from old 'ABC' Cunningham for Gertie and his observer; just six foot of Italian earth.

'So that leaves Clarke and Green of the first strike missing,' the Intelligence officer said a little wearily, rising to his feet to meet those returning from the second strike who were due back soon. 'All right, you dozy lot, go and grab your bacon and eggs in the wardroom. Hurry up about it, you dozy lot.

Then get some sleep. They'll probably ask you to do it again tonight.'

'Christ,' a weary pilot ran his hand through his tousled hair, 'they only asked the Light Brigade to do it once.'

Boyd was personally reporting the details to a tired Admiral Lyster when the signal came in from old 'ABC. It was stilted but traditional. It read, *'Illustrious* manoeuvre well executed'.

Lyster laughed shortly. 'Old "ABC" doesn't go overboard with his praise, does he, eh? We knock out a large chunk of the Italian navy and that's all the praise we get.' He shrugged and his face grew serious again, 'What are you going to do about Clarke and Green, Boyd?' he rasped.

It was a problem that had been troubling the captain ever since the second strike had landed and had reported they had seen no sign of the missing 'stringbag'. But he answered promptly enough, though he knew his reply wouldn't be to the Admiral's liking. 'Keep on station at Y for Yorker till daybreak, then re-join old "ABC" and the fleet.'

Lyster frowned. 'You know the Eyeties will be out looking for us soon in their scores, perhaps in their hundreds. Old Musso will be burning to take revenge. You understand that, don't you?'

'I do,' Boyd replied firmly, knowing that it was the Navy's tradition that the captain of the ship made the decisions about his own ship even when he had a higher-ranking officer sailing with him. 'I feel I owe it to those brave young men. As soon as we sail at daybreak then I come under the orders of the C.-in-C., old "ABC" Cunningham and the decision will be taken out of my hands.' He flashed a look at his wristwatch. 'First light will be about zero seven hundred. Clarke and Green have till then with us remaining at this station.'

The Admiral's frown deepened. He knew Boyd was risking the Fleet's only functioning aircraft carrier in the Mediterranean and a crew of over a thousand. Still he *was* the captain of the *Illustrious*. 'All right, Boyd,' he said finally. 'Do it your way.' He yawned. 'I'm off to my cabin to get a bit of shut-eye. See I'm wakened if anything develops before dawn.' Lyster's intent was obvious and now it was Captain Boyd's turn to frown. But aloud he said, 'I will, sir. Good night, sir.'

The Admiral turned and left the bridge, leaving Boyd with his thoughts. They were not happy ones and a moment later his gloom deepened even more as the first lieu-tenant in charge of the carrier's six Fulmar seaborne fighters called him on the bridge with, 'Sir, radar's just sighted two enemy planes. Radar thinks they're Italian seaplanes on account of their speed.'

'Looking for us?'

'That's my guess, sir.'

'All right scramble. Knock them out of the sky before they can get within sighting dis-tance of the *Illustrious*.'

'Yes, sir,' the young airman answered happily. The 'stringbag' wallahs had been having all the fun so far. Now it was the turn of the fighters. The phone went dead.

Minutes later the first of the Fulmars were roaring away from the carrier heading for the north-west where the Italian reconnais-sance planes had been sighted.

Now it was an hour till first light and Boyd could still not bring himself to go to his bunk and have a sleep, though he had not slept for nearly twenty-four hours now. Down below in the hangar, the riggers and the mechanics were working all-out to patch up and get ready the 'stringbags'. Fifteen of them were going to attack Taranto again that night and a worried Boyd knew that the Italians would be waiting for them this time.

The weather was worsening, too. The barometer was falling rapidly. Low cloud was coming in fast and the sea had turned very choppy. Flying off the heaving, tossing flight deck in weather like this was going to be tricky. Boyd knew that, and he didn't want to sacrifice any more of his young aircrew. The Fleet Air Arm had had two bites at the cherry. Why not let the Royal Air Force bombers stationed at Malta have a go at Taranto now?

Half an hour before first light the chief yeoman of signals came on to the bridge, grinning and bearing a message. 'For you, sir, from the fighter commander.'

'Read it,' Boyd snapped; he had left his spectacles in his cabin.

'Ay, ay, sir.' The yeoman unfolded the flimsy note and read it out, hardly able to conceal his excitement. 'Both sorties successful. We knocked the Eyeties for six.'

Boyd breathed a sigh of relief, 'That's put paid to their recce planes at least.'

'Yes sir,' the yeoman agreed and Boyd told himself the news would be all over the ship in half an hour's time. But that was no bad thing. It would ease the crew's tension till dawn when they would sail to rejoin the fleet.

'And sir,' the yeoman said.

'Yes?'

'The cipher officer told me that a message is coming in from the C.-in-C. For your eyes only. He's busy at the moment decoding, sir.'

'Thank you. Get the cipher officer to bring it to me immediately.'

'Ay, ay, sir.' The yeoman saluted and went.

Five minutes later Boyd had Cunningham's message. It was the second piece of cheering news he had read in that long, pre-dawn wait. Cunningham signalled: 'I am relying on your judgement to give up the operation tonight if for any reason you feel it is not feasible or if it is asking too much of the Fleet Air Arm. I am as anxious as you and they are to put the finishing touch on last night's fine effort, but don't allow this to bias your judgement.'

Again Boyd sighed with relief. That effectively let his tired young airmen off the hook. Now there was only a question of the missing plane with Clarke and Green. He looked at his watch and pinched the bridge of his nose, realising for the first time just how tired he was. He frowned. The two men had just thirty minutes left...

SEVEN

Mussolini sat alone in the great office, brooding. It was still not dawn and there was little sound from the city outside – the stamp of the sentries' boots on the cobbles, a faint rattle of a horse and cart, bringing in milk from the country for the Romans, the jingling of the trams heading for the main railway station. All the familiar sounds that he had become accustomed to in the eighteen years that he had been using this office.

Yet this day they seemed strange, unreal. Everything did. He was not by nature an imaginative man. Politicians didn't need that kind of imagination, especially dictators who, as he had always maintained to his fascist cronies, had to have 'closed hearts'. But now his imagination seemed to be running away with him. Everything seemed strange, different, changed.

Two hours before when he had been awakened from his sleep and had been told what had happened at Taranto, he had flown into a great rage, as his fearful staff had expected him to. Naked save for his slippers, he had burst into Clara's bedroom, pulled the silken sheets off her nubile body, ripped up her nightdress and had flung himself upon her, already erect. He had taken her silently, savagely, without a word, until she was groaning and moaning whether from fear or pleasure he had not known nor cared.

Soaked in sweat and panting for breath as if he had just run a great race, but satisfied, he had left her sprawled on the rumpled silk sheets without a word and had gone – still naked – to his office. He had picked up the telephone and called the *Comando Supremo*. As he waited for the connection with the chief of the *Regia Aeronautica*, the Italian Air Force, his brain raced electrically. Sooner or later the British, with their reconnaissance flights, would discover that they had knocked out three Italian capital ships, plus numerous other craft. Naturally Churchill in London would attempt to make much propaganda out of it. He badly needed a victory to counteract the defeat at Dunkirk. But if he could beat Churchill to it with a victory of his own, that would lessen the impact of the destruction of the Italian fleet.

Finally the head of the Air Force came to

the phone, spluttering apologies and making excuses for the delay.

The *Duce* cut him short with a curt, 'Our Air Force raided London last night. What are the results? What are the casualties? How many British planes did we shoot down?'

Mussolini heard the Air Force general gulp audibly at the other end of the line. 'Come on, out with it,' he barked.

'Bad news, *Duce*,' the general said hesitantly, for he knew many heads were going to roll this day, and he didn't want his to be one of them.

'How bad?' Mussolini demanded.

'We sent in twenty bombers escorted by sixty fighters,' the General paused momentarily, then the rest of the sentence came out in a rush, 'Eight bombers and five fighters were shot down by the treacherous British.'

Mussolini could have moaned out loud. He caught himself just in time. The new Roman never showed any weak emotions. 'I see,' he said carefully, knowing he could make no propaganda with this first Italian raid on London. 'All right, another question. What has the Air Force done to find the English carrier from which the raid on Taranto was launched, eh?'

'I have two hundred and fifty aircraft on

red alert at this very moment, *Duce,*' the General announced proudly. 'Ah, but why on red alert you may ask, *Duce,*' the General said, pre-empting the impatient dictator. 'I shall tell you.'

'Pray do,' Mussolini said mildly, rolling those dark eyes of his as he always did when he wanted to show that he was dealing with some madman or other.

'Because, *Duce,* we have not found the British ships as yet. Two of our reconnaissance flying boats have been shot down in the attempt, but we have others airborne, searching for the perfidious British. You can rest assured, sir that the British will be found.'

'They will have to be this morning,' Mussolini snapped. 'If you wish to retain your post.' He slammed the phone down without another word.

But he was not really angry, more apprehensive. As he slumped there at his great desk, heavy unshaven chin clasped in both hands, listening to the sounds of Rome beginning to wake up, he could see quite clearly what might happen now. The rest of the Italian Fleet would have to move to the shelter of Naples on the west coast. That would mean they would not be able to support Marshal Graziani in Egypt. He knew Graziani. He would whine and moan and maintain he couldn't move deeper into Egypt unless the Italian Navy guaranteed his seaborne supplies. His advance on Cairo, which he had boasted would break British rule in North Africa, would bog down.

There'd be trouble supporting his armies engaged in fighting the Greeks. That would hearten Athens and it wouldn't be long before the English would be landing troops in Greece to help their new allies.

Suddenly, crushingly, all the great hopes he had cherished since June when he had attacked France after the Germans had broken the power of the French Army and chased the British from the Continent, vanished. What could he do. Where could he find help? Could he appeal to Hitler? If he did, he knew what would happen: he would become the junior party in the fascist alliance, the second man in a movement which he had created. Hitler, not he, would dominate Europe. Those same barbarians who had destroyed the old Roman Empire and had once sacked Rome, would be in control again, not his new Romans.

He felt a cold finger of fear trace its way down his spine. The future abruptly looked black and uncertain.

The great door opened. He felt the sudden draught. He looked up, his unshaven face tragic and broken. It was Clara. She was clad in only a sheer white silk dressing gown, which was open to reveal her tanned body. '*Caro,*' she cried, recognising the look of near despair on his face. She ran towards him, great breasts trembling beneath the sheer material.

She seized his head in both hands and pressed it against her naked breasts. For a moment he rested his head thus, the tears beginning to well up in his dark eyes. She freed one hand and pulled out her left breast with its large, dull-brown nipple. Like a fond mother feeding a beloved child, she pressed the nipple gently into his mouth. Greedily he began to suck on it, the tears flowing down his cheeks unhindered. She patted his bald pate soothingly. 'There … there,' she whispered. 'Nothing can happen to you now, baby. There … there.'

'The New Caesar', as he had once called himself proudly, nodded his head and continued to suckle greatly, as if his whole life depended upon it.

Time passed. How long neither of them ever knew afterwards. But it was thus, with

Clara's nipple pressed between the *Duce's* greedy lips, that the telephone caught and disturbed them with its insistent ringing. For an age, neither of them seemed to notice. The *Duce* was too intent on his task, like a greedy baby that could not get enough of his mother's milk, and Clara, like a mother too besotted with the task of feeding her new baby, to hear.

Finally Clara released him from her grasp. Reluctantly he took his lips from her breast. 'The telephone,' she said dreamily.

Reluctantly the *Duce* took his mouth away from her nipple. 'What?' he asked in a child-like voice.

Again she patted his bald pate. 'The telephone, baby,' she whispered. 'It's ringing.'

'Oh yes.' With a shaky hand and still holding tightly to her left breast, with his other hand he reached for the receiver. Shakily he held it to his ear, but said nothing.

'*Duce... Duce,* is that you?' It was the commander of the Air Force.

He did not answer. He seemed in a state of shock. Again the Air Force general asked, 'Is that you, *Duce?* Please answer, sir, it is vitally important.' There was a note of pleading in the other man's voice.

Finally Mussolini said, his voice very low

and without emotion. 'It is I, Mussolini.'

'Thank God, sir,' the general cried. 'I have great news, sir.'

'What?'

'We have found one of them. A straggler. It will lead us right to the enemy fleet.'

Mussolini looked bewildered. 'I do ... I do not understand,' he stuttered.

The general repeated what he had just said and added, 'It is one of the attacking planes, lagging behind the others. It appears to have some sort of engine trouble. One of our planes is shadowing it and is in constant radio contact with headquarters. Once it spots the English fleet, we attack. Isn't that great news, *Duce?*'

'Yes,' Mussolini said weakly. Then he pulled himself together with a sheer effort of naked willpower and forced some iron into his voice. 'You will inform me immediately, General, when the attack against the English fleet commences. Do you understand, General?'

'*Si, Duce!*' the general snapped. 'At once, sir.' The phone went dead.

Clara looked at his worn, tear-stained face. 'Good news?' she asked hopefully.

He shrugged in that eloquent manner of his. 'I suppose,' he said carelessly. 'But what does it matter? It will not stave off the inevitable.'

'What do you mean, Benito?... The inevitable?'

By way of an answer, he said, his voice weak and ineffectual, 'You must leave me, Clara.'

'*Leave you?*'

'Yes, before it is too late. I do not want to drag you down with me. I am an old man. I can accept what fate brings. I have lived a life. But you are nearly thirty years younger than I. You have a life to live, children to bear, a right to live … to enjoy.'

She stared at him incredulously. She had never heard Benito speak before like this. She knew he had other women and undoubtedly he took them like he took her, brutally, selfishly. That very sexual brutality had been one of the things that had attracted him to her right from the start. She liked to be taken, to be mastered by a man. She wanted none of those empty words about love and romance. She desired brutal, direct, masculine sexuality. Now her lover seemed suddenly weak and old, his charisma vanished.

'Yes,' he continued as if he could not see the look of alarm, shock on her beautiful face. 'The Italian people are not the new

295

Romans. They are a corrupt, venial people. All they want is food, money, an easy time. They will betray me. Whatever happens now,' he said with a note of finality in his voice, 'they will in the end betray me...'

EIGHT

Dawn.

A blood-red sun hung on the edge of the sea to the east, colouring the water a sinister scarlet. The sea itself was flat, motionless. Not a wave stirred. All was empty, brooding, sinister.

Gamely the battered Swordfish chugged on, its radial engine occasionally giving off frightening coughs and splutters. But as yet it had not missed a stroke and Clarke noted with some satisfaction that he still had a quarter of a tank of petrol left. That would be quite enough to get him to the rendez-vous 'Y for Yorker'.

He took up the Gosport tube. 'Is the bastard still there, Gino?' he croaked, for he was unutterably weary. He had coaxed the damaged plane at just above stalling speed along all night and the strain was telling. And then there had been the business of their 'shadow'.

About two hours before dawn Gino had announced its presence, 'George,' he had said urgently over the Gosport, 'there's a plane behind us.'

'One of ours?' he had asked, knowing even as he had posed the question that that eventuality was hardly likely. All the Swordfishes that were coming back to the carrier would already have done so.

'No, Eyetie,' Gino had replied. 'By the look of it, a Fiat fighter, as far as I can make out.'

So the 'shadow' had entered their lonely little world. Twice Clarke had throttled back as far as he dared in order that the fighter should catch up with them. Then they would have a crack at it with Gino's rear cockpit machine gun. But the Fiat fighter had remained obstinately behind them. It wasn't going to be lured. Once he had pushed the old battered plane as far as he dared. The Fiat had increased speed too and had kept up, but always out of shooting range.

'You know his game, don't you, George?' Gino said now.

'I can guess, but you tell me, Gino.'

'He's tailing us till we get to the *Illustrious*. Then he will signal back to the Eyeties' bases on the mainland. Then the wop air force will be on to the carrier like frigging bees around the frigging honey pot. The old *Illustrious* won't stand chance. The old ship will be fighting against the whole of the Eyetie air force.'

George Clarke thought for a moment. He knew Gino was right. The Italian fighter would have attacked him long ago, if it had intended to do so. It had the speed and fire power, much more than the old 'stringbag' had. Besides the fighter would soon be getting to the limit of its range. Why risk coming down in the drink when it could have its 'kill' now?'

'What do you think we should do, Gino?' he asked, knowing even as he spoke that he couldn't lead the Italian to the carrier. That would be unthinkable. Not only would that place Britain's only effective carrier in the Med. at risk, but also the lives of some one thousand fellow seamen.

Gino answered by posing a question of his own. 'What about trying to set down on the airfield at that Greek island Ceph-thing-a-me bob?'

'Cephalonia? Don't think we could make

it with the fuel we've got left, Gino,' George said after a quick glance at the fuel gauge.

'Then we've got to knock the bastard out of the sky,' Gino said grimly with sudden determination. 'That's going to be the way of it.'

'Of course, you're right,' George agreed heartily, new strength in his voice. 'We've got to get the bastard to fight and with a bit of luck we'll nail him. But how?'

'Well, obviously he's not going to fall for the old rear cockpit surprise, as that Macchi did,' Gino said. 'We've got to do it with the forward machine gun. That's our only chance.'

'Agreed.'

'So, you can see George that we're flying into the sun. Makes seeing things difficult.'

'Agreed again.'

'So what if you did a tight turn and came right at him? For a few seconds you'd have the advantage of him coming in from the sun while he's squinting in at it. With a bit of luck, you might just get the bastard. If you don't and he lets us have it and we get the chop, then we've got the 'chutes. We can bail out, call a "Mayday" and wait for air sea rescue from that Greek island to come and pick us up. The Med. is as smooth as glass and visibility is good. We've got a pretty good chance of being picked up before the day is out.' Gino licked his parched lips after so much talking and added, 'It's the only way I can see of not shopping the *Illustrious*.'

'We'll do it,' George said boldly, his mind made up. 'I think we've got a fighting chance.'

Gino laughed a little wildly and said over the Gosport tube. 'Roll on death, George, and let's have a go at the frigging angels.'

Carefully George Clarke started to throttle back, eyes glued to his instruments, cutting the speed carefully, face set and tense. For a few moments their 'shadow' didn't notice the plane in front of it. Then it did and started to reduce speed as well. All the same the distance between them was now much less and in the rear cockpit, Gino said excitedly, 'I reckon there's only about three hundred feet between us now, George.'

'Yes,' Clarke answered laconically. He was concentrating now totally on what he had to do. All the advantages were on the side of the Italian. The only one that he had was surprise. 'All right, Gino, listen to this. Count ten and give him a burst. I know you won't hit him at that range, but you'll rattle him. In the same moment that you open up,

300

I'll go for him. Got it?'

'Got it.'

'Right, start counting.'

Behind him, Gino seized the single machine gun, cocked it and began to count. *'One ... two ... three ... four...'*

Clarke wiped the sweat off his brow with the back of his hand. He cocked and armed his own single machine gun. He prayed he wouldn't have a stoppage at the crucial moment. He counted, too, *'Six ... seven ... eight...'*

'Nine ... ten!' Gino Green barked and pressed the trigger. Tracer began to curve towards the unsuspecting Italian fighter like a line of glowing golfballs, arcing upwards and then, as Clarke had guessed, dropping slightly short of the Fiat. But the pilot was rattled. He could see that in the rear-view mirror. It was his opportunity. He broke to port. The 'stringbag' groaned and squeaked at the sudden strain. The perspiration running in channels down his face, he forced the Swordfish around in a tight turn. With all his strength he pushed the throttle forward.

Now the Swordfish was hurtling forward at nearly a hundred knots heading on a collision course for the Italian plane. *Three hundred feet ... two hundred and fifty ... two*

301

hundred... In the glare of the dawn sun, harsh and blood-red, Clarke could see every detail of the fast Italian fighter – the oil smears at the engine, the line of rivets along the cowling, the white face of the helmeted pilot... *One hundred feet.* It was now or never. The Italian pilot would break off at any second. 'Take this you bastard,' Clarke cried, tense with excitement, and pressed the trigger.

Nothing!

He pressed the trigger again, squeezing furiously.

Again – *nothing!*

It was in that fleeting second that George Clarke made his awesome, overwhelming decision. 'Gino,' he yelled wildly, 'I'm going to ram him. It's the only way. Hold on to your hat!'

Gino crossed himself. With luck they'd be able to bale out, but he wasn't so sure. Hurriedly, as the plane surged forward, he started to mutter the 'Act of Contrition'.

Madly the Italian pilot, his eyes bulging out of his head like those of a man demented, tried to break as the ancient biplane filled the whole world in front of him. To no avail. He screamed shrilly. There was an awesome rending-tearing crash. The canopy disappeared. The pilot felt the joystick skewer his chest, pinning him to his seat for all eternity. Next moment the crippled fighter's fuel tank exploded. With a great whooshing roar, it went up in flames. Like a gigantic blowtorch the flame seared the length of the Swordfish.

Clarke screamed shrilly and flung up his arms to protect his face. To no avail. The all-consuming flame devoured him. He screamed and died an instant later. In the same moment that a desperate Gino jumped, the two planes, locked together in an embrace of death, fell out of the sky. They tumbled down, shedding bits and pieces of metal, trailing a cloud of smoke and fire. A second later they hit the sea with a tremendous splash. They went under instantly, leaving the sea behind them hissing and seething, as if in resentment.

Slowly, sadly, Gino Green drifted down, the wind howling through holes scorched in his parachute. His eyes flashing back and forth searching the surface of the sea below for any sign of George.

But all he saw was the pathetic litter of the wreckage – a cork life-belt, an empty boot, what looked like a bottle bobbing down and up on the faint swell. George Clarke had vanished for good.

Gino Green was barely conscious when the Air Sea Rescue launch from Malta finally found him floating alone in the sea and in great pain from his burns. But as the RAF sergeant at the wheel sang out, 'All right, Navy we're here,' he opened his eyes slowly and said in a weak voice, with just a note of his old defiance in it. 'But we scuppered the Eyetie sods, that we did … we beat 'em.' Then as they lifted him gently onto the white-painted launch, everything went black and he slipped into the blessed oblivion of unconsciousness... 'Operation Judgement' was over.

NINE

Winston Churchill was tremendously excited. Outside another daylight raid was taking place over London. Fighters snarled, the ack-ack guns barked and German Heinkels scuttled across the capital, dropping their bombs as they fled for the sea. None of this worried the new Prime Minister one bit. He sat at his desk, cigar jutting from the side of his mouth, a large whisky and soda at his side, scribbling away, scratching out, re-writing, working against time, for the first session of the House of Commons was only minutes away; and all the while he threw his comments at young John Colville, his secretary.

'This will rub old Musso's nose in it,' he said cheerfully, adding another few words with a flourish of his fountain pen. 'The First Sea Lord is a queer fish. I congratulated him on the Taranto affair, but he said the praise was due to Cunningham. But in fairness to Pound', he meant the First Sea Lord, 'I must say that I suggested it to him the other day and he telegraphed the plan out to Cunningham.'

Colville grinned to himself. As always the PM was a great egoist. Now he thought the plan for 'Operation Judgement' had been his all along. But it didn't matter. It had been a great victory.

With a final flourish, a sip of his whisky and a puff at the cigar Churchill announced, as he rose to his feet, 'Well that's done. Let's hie to the House, John, and tell them about our great victory.'

Ten minutes later Churchill was standing up in front of a packed House of Commons, paper in hand, peering at the MPs through his pebble glasses consummate showman that he was, letting them wait for his news. Finally he cleared his throat and rasped, 'I have some news for the House. It is good news. The Royal Navy has struck a crippling blow to the Italian Fleet.'

The House erupted into wild cheering. MPs threw their order papers in the air. Others slapped one another on the back in delight. This was the first British victory since the country entered the war over a year before.

Churchill let them have their fun before clearing his throat noisily once more and continuing. 'The total battleship strength of the Italian Fleet was six, two of the *Littorio* class, which had just been put into service and are, of course, among the most powerful vessels in the world, and four of the recently reconstructed *Cavour* class.'

'This fleet was, of course, considerably more powerful on paper than our own Mediterranean Fleet, but it had consistently refused to accept battle.' The Prime Minister looked over the tops of his spectacles to make sure they realised just how contemptible he thought the Italians for not sailing out to fight. Then he went on, 'On the night of November 11-12th when the main units of the Italian Fleet were lying behind their shore defences in their naval base at Taranto, our aircraft of the Fleet Air Arm attacked them in their stronghold.' He paused and made the MPs wait.

'Now the reports of our airmen have been confirmed by photographic reconnaissance. It is now established that one battleship of the *Littorio* class is badly down by the bows, that her forecastle is under water and she has a heavy list to port.'

There were cheers from the members, but Churchill pushed on without pause, as if he were very excited personally by the news he was now reading out to them.

'One battleship of the *Cavour* class has been beached and her stern, up to and including the after turret, is under water. This ship is also heavily listed to starboard.'

Churchill took a sip of water from the glass in front of him and continued. 'It has not yet been possible to establish the fact with certainty, but it appears possible that a second battleship of the *Cavour* class has also been severely damaged and beached.'

'In the inner harbour of Taranto two Italian cruisers are listed to starboard and are surrounded by oil fuel and two Fleet auxiliaries are lying with their sterns under water...'

Churchill beamed at his great audience, 'I feel it my duty to bring this glorious episode–' His words were interrupted by wild cheering and the Prime Minister waited patiently, allowing the MPs this outbreak of emotion, as a tolerant head might after he had announced the first eleven had just won an important match, '–to the immediate notice of the House,' he continued after a few moments. 'As a result of a determined and highly successful attack, which reflects the greatest honour on the Fleet Air Arm, only three of the Italian battleships remain effective.'

Churchill looked suddenly sombre. Why, he could not reason at the time, but just over a year later on December 7th, 1941, he would know why. 'This result,' he went on, 'while it affects decisively the balance of naval power in the Mediterranean, also carries with it reactions upon the naval situation in other quarters of the globe.'

If the six hundred-odd MPs present were puzzled by the reference, they did not show it. As Churchill folded his paper and took off his spectacles to indicate his announcement was finished, they rose to their feet as one. Wild cheering broke out, hands were clapped. MPs shouted, 'Good Old Winnie!' Someone cried, 'Three cheers for the Fleet Air Arm!'

Then as the ushers came into the chamber, stamping their rods and calling, 'Gentlemen, another air raid warning has been sounded. Gentlemen, will you pray attend to the air raid shelters,' the euphoria vanished and the MPs knew it was just another day in a long grey war. Obediently they started to file out to the shelters, leaving Churchill there alone, momentarily, wondering how this great victory – the destruction of a fleet from the air – was going to influence the future course of naval warfare...

At the other side of the globe, big burly Admiral Yamamoto, C.-in-C. of the Imperial Japanese Navy thought he already knew. He nodded to the aide who had been translating the broadcast from the London BBC and he switched off the radio promptly. The big bald Admiral was not one to tolerate the slightest delay.

Yamamoto grunted in that slow, deliberate, ponderous manner of his and looked across the big table under the whirling ceiling fan at Admiral Nagumo. 'Well, what do you think?' he barked.

The Admiral, dapper and small, shifted his samurai sword to a more comfortable position and answered, 'Well, now we can see that it can be done. The British have shown us that at Taranto.'

'Agreed. It has always been my contention that Japan must deal the US Navy a fatal blow at the outset of war,' Yamamoto growled in that ponderous manner of his, as if every word had to be considered carefully before it was uttered. 'Destroy the American fleet right at the outset and we have a free hand in our military operations. Naturally we shall have a much longer approach flight than the British.'

Nagumo answered at once, 'We are already training our crews at refuelling at sea. That will double the radius of any task force.'

'Good.' That was high praise coming from such a dour man as Admiral Yamamoto.

'My initial thoughts are these,' Nagumo said. 'We must surprise the Americans. Attack, say, on a Sunday morning, early. Everyone knows the Americans are useless on a Sunday morning. They're mostly still drunk from the night before.'

There were little giggles from the other staff officer and even the bull-like Admiral gave a careful wintry smile.

'We use the same technique as the English at Taranto. A double strike, with the second force coming in soon after the first.'

Yamamoto nodded his agreement.

'There will be some differences. Our strike force will be composed of three type of aircraft, not two as with the British. In addition to torpedo bombers and normal bombers, we shall have fighters, the Zero, to protect them.'

Again the C.-in-C. nodded his approval.

'In addition to our new torpedoes, we are converting 16-inch armour-piercing shells into bombs for our bombers. Thus every ship struck, either by a torpedo or a shell-bomb will undoubtedly sink,' Nagumo said proudly. 'Unlike the British at Taranto, we shall sink the *whole* of the American Fleet!'

'Good.' Yamamoto clapped his hands. As if by magic, an aide appeared at the door of the wardroom with a silver tray filled with cups of *saki*. With a bow and swift intake of air up his nostrils to indicate his respect of each of the high ranking staff officers present, he handed them each a cup of the rice wine.

Yamamoto waited till each officer had one. Then he held up his cup in toast. 'To victory at Pearl Harbour!' he bellowed, yellow face

311

suddenly red as if with fury. '*Banzai!*'

'To victory at Pearl Harbour!' they roared back. '*Banzai!*' They drained their glasses as one and then flung them at the wardroom wall where they smashed into splinters, as if to symbolise that the deed was done.

A second Taranto was in the planning. But this one would shake and change the world...

It's now well over half a century since we went in at Taranto, on that attack which did, indeed, change the whole course of the war against Italy. It helped to accelerate the defeat of Marshal Graziani's Italian Army in Egypt so that Hitler had to send in the 'Desert Fox', Rommel, to help bale the Italians out. But in the end the Axis powers were kicked out of Africa and as Mussolini had predicted after the Taranto attack, the Italian people turned against him in July 1943. Two years later he was dead. Shot by his own people, his body was vilely desecrated by his 'new Romans'. They strung him and his mistress, Clara Petacci up by their feet and urinated into their dead mouths. Not only men, but women as well!

But most of those brave young pilots and observers who had helped in November

1940 to bring about the ultimate fall of the Italian dictator never lived to see that event. The fierce aerial battles which raged in the Mediterranean between 1940 and 1943 and later in the Pacific against the Japs took their toll. Most of them died young in battle with their 'blood hot', as old Winnie Churchill used to say.

Nor were they really much honoured at the time. I recall one of my fellow aircrew snorting in December 1941 after the Pearl Harbour fiasco, 'The bloody Nips ought to give us all a gong. After all we *did* show 'em how to do it at Taranto last year.' Not that the pilots and observers who took part in the great attack were ever awarded much in the way of honours from His Majesty's Government.

In fact, immediately after the attack, only *two* medals were awarded to the whole 1,000 odd strong crew of the *Illustrious*. The ship's company were so hurt and incensed that they vented their feelings by tearing down the notice board copies of the Fleet Orders in which the announcement was made.

Six months later, the Admiralty tried to make up by sending out a couple of extra gongs to the Med. for the flying crews. Yet not one officer or rating who had worked so bloody hard to get the strike planes ready for action at Taranto was ever acknowledged, though this was a 'battle' and not a mere 'raid'.

Indeed the Taranto attack had been, as we can see today, a decisive turning point in the history of naval warfare. Those obsolete 'stringbags' had inflicted more damage on an enemy fleet in ten minutes than the whole British Grand Fleet had done on the German Navy at the battle of Jutland back in 1916. That's why there is no European Navy with a battleship in its fleet today. We showed the world just how vulnerable battleships were to air attack.

No matter. It's a long time ago now. Who should still feel the bitterness of that year when just a handful of us were instrumental in starting the downfall of the Italian dictator? We did it, and that's an achievement in itself – with or without gongs.

Thereafter, the old *Illustrious* fought a long and bitter war. More than once she was nearly written off by the enemy. She survived though; she was a tough old bastard! In the end it was the knackers who did for her. She was scrapped in 1956 and there was many a tear shed by the survivors when they saw her go. For a long time there was no new *Illustrious*.

Today there is. Proudly that *Illustrious* carries on her scroll, the one battle honour that to the Fleet Air Arm will always remain supreme, as long as there is a Fleet Air Arm. It is 'TARANTO'.

Vice-Admiral G Green,
DSO, DSC, OBE, RN (Retd)
Stringbag House, Gosport, Summer 1994.

The publishers hope that this book has given you enjoyable reading. Large Print Books are especially designed to be as easy to see and hold as possible. If you wish a complete list of our books please ask at your local library or write directly to:

Magna Large Print Books
Magna House, Long Preston,
Skipton, North Yorkshire.
BD23 4ND

This Large Print Book, for people
who cannot read normal print,
is published under the auspices of

THE ULVERSCROFT FOUNDATION

... we hope you have enjoyed this book.
Please think for a moment about those
who have worse eyesight than you ...
and are unable to even read or enjoy
Large Print without great difficulty.

You can help them by sending a
donation, large or small, to:

**The Ulverscroft Foundation,
1, The Green, Bradgate Road,
Anstey, Leicestershire, LE7 7FU,
England.**
or request a copy of our brochure for
more details.

The Foundation will use all donations
to assist those people who are visually
impaired and need special attention
with medical research, diagnosis
and treatment.

Thank you very much for your help.